# SECONDS

Internet Famous Collection, 6

## CAM JOHNS

Copyright © 2020 by Cam Johns
All rights reserved. No part of this book may be reproduced or transmitted in any form or by any means, electronic or mechanical, including photocopying, recording, or by any information storage and retrieval system, without permission in writing from copyright owner.

This is a work of fiction. Names, characters, places and incidents either are the product of the author's imagination or are used fictitiously, and any resemblance to any actual persons, living or dead, events or locales is entirely coincidental.

www.thecamjohns.com
thecamjohns@gmail.com
Developmental Edits by: Dr. Plot Twist
Proofreading: Dominique Laura
Cover Design: Touch Creations

## PROLOGUE

### Turmoil

My ears are flooded with the noises spewing from the intercom, frustrating my subconscious. The constant borage of feet pattering along the halls, totally disregarding my belligerent sobbing, only encourages the anger slowly building within me. Sobbing that becomes obnoxiously louder, the more I think of her smile. Her embrace. Her soft touch against my thick, hardened exterior.

A touch that will never be felt again.

All because of choices I made. Decisions that kept me from being by her side and bringing us here—a place I'll never return to. Full of saddened, lonely people, facing life-altering decisions. Just as I have. A decision that has been taken from me because we weren't married yet.

I stare at the velvet, red ring box I hadn't had a chance to give her, and never will because her heartless fucking parents made that irrevocable decision to pull the plug. Exiling my pleas to hold off and give her more time. More time to fight ... for her life ... for us ... for me. But, those pieces of shits don't even acknowledge my need to keep her alive.

Granted, they hadn't known about my presence until recently. But, regardless of what the doctors say, they are not always right. They can be wrong. However, as it turns out, they are all against me. I am the one that's wrong.

Well, fuck them! Fuck their judgments. Fuck their forsaken attitudes. Fuck their cavalier convictions. Fuck. Them.

I slowly peel myself up from the hospital floor, wiping the remaining tears from my face and ignoring the dampness of my torn T-shirt. I stand across from her room, staring through the glass, watching her life drain from her body. Her parents lie across their daughter, crying just as hard as I am on the outside.

But I know what lies beneath those outlying emotions. Emotions I learned were false over the past year. Emotions that propelled their daughter directly into my arms. And what signed her DNR, in my opinion. But they'll get what's coming to them. One way or another. Even if it takes my own knife-wielding hands.

## CHAPTER ONE

### My Destroyer

*3 Years Ago ...*

"Dammit!" I push Sen's head down into the pillow, making her arch her back more and stay put. Clearly, she's becoming weaker, but that shit is just pissing me off. "Don't fuckin' move."

I thrust into the woman I'm doing for the moment faster, wanting to nut so I can get her the fuck out of my room. The pillow muffles her carnal screams as sweat begins to drip down my face. I've never really worked this hard to get off, but today was a shitty-ass day, and I need this. I need my dick deep inside some random's pussy for as long as my body can stand. Which is longer than hers, apparently, because her voluptuous legs are trembling.

I concentrate harder on getting off so I can stop manhandling her. Though, I know that's what she appreciates most about our impromptu sex life. Letting her head go, I grab at her hips and pound into her as the smacking noises of our bodies clashing together echo through the hotel bedroom.

Her legs succumb to the impact, so I have no choice but to pick them up and wrap them at my hips. *Hmm*, my dick goes in much deeper now. "Fuck!" I shout, finally letting go of the built-up tension from the day. It turns out opening a restaurant is tedious work. If people would just do what the fuck I say in the first place, I wouldn't be so annoyed right now.

I immediately stand, releasing my grip on her thighs, and she falls to the bed. *God, I hope she doesn't think she's staying.* I'm tired of being that guy. That guy who pretends not to give a fuck so chicks don't get attached. No matter how many times I meet someone and admit I'm not looking for a relationship, they always think they can change my mind or some shit. It's pretty ridiculous and a complete turnoff. I'd rather be told to go fuck myself, but women never tell me that. I don't know if it has something to do with my career, the money, my looks, or whatever. No clue. But I know I'm an asshole.

I don't want to be one, but I'm tired of being used. Used for sex, money, connections I may have ... I'm just not going to be hurt again. I refuse to.

After pulling off the condom and flushing it down the toilet, I look in the mirror to clean off all the sweat that has pebbled on my face and chest. *I need a damn haircut,* I think while staring at my getting-out-of-control goatee and growing hair.

Suddenly, Sen's hands come across my stomach and start to massage my chest. I guess she's found the strength in her legs again. *Fuck me.* I let her do her silly cuddling thing as I wipe my face clean, trying to ignore the effect I've allowed this particular woman to have on my body. I don't know what it is about her, but her touch always gets me to do shit my mind doesn't want to.

In fact, she hasn't been *a random woman* for a few months now. I consciously ignore the butterflies that flutter within my stomach the more she rubs her hands on my chest, as she lays her head on my dampened back. I turn off the guy I wish I could be and remain the asshole I need to be.

"That was fun," she whispers, letting her hands slither down my six-pack, to my semi-hard dick. She gazes at my chocolate skin, then softly kisses my chest, making me want to melt for her right then and there.

*I'm really not in the mood for this shit.* But I have to turn the sensitivity off. I spin around, leaning my butt on the sink, cross my arms at my chest, and kiss her on the forehead. "Do you need me to pay for your Uber?" I ask, cupping her cheeks in my hands.

She eyes me curiously as if she hadn't expected me to say that, which I don't get because I never let her spend the night. We've been doing this booty call thing for a few months longer than I usually allow. I've never let her know I consider her more than I care to admit.

I can't let her get any closer to me. My mistake is occasionally dating her whenever I'm in town to oversee the opening of my second restaurant here in Maryland. But today, she asked if I would like to come to one of her family's Sunday dinners again, so I know she's getting way too close. I'd rather not let her know I plan to move here and build on this particular restaurant. Something in my gut tells me I need to be here.

She backs away from me suddenly and goes into the bedroom area. I hear her fumbling around and realize I've upset her. Not so surprising. I saunter into the room and lean against the wall adjacent to the doorway of the bathroom, watching her frustration build as she hurriedly tries to find all of her clothing that I threw all over the place trying to fuck her. It took her all of five minutes to finally get her shit on.

*It was like an eternity*. The longer she remains in my presence, the harder it is to suppress the guy inside that just wants to pull her into my chest and tell her how beautiful I think she is. My eyes reluctantly follow her around the room, as I contemplate asking her to stay. She's not a bad person, and she's absolutely gorgeous. Her eyes have captivated me since day one and continue to break down my walls.

But I'm just not ready.

Not ready to be tied down, not ready to start a relationship and be a family man ... or let my heart be destroyed again. I'm just not there. I'm twenty-five, and I only needed to get cheated on once for my heart to turn to stone. That stone has only cemented further, nothing else. If I were a different person, I might have given her a chance—given *this* a chance.

"Do you need me to walk you out?" I ask, still leaning in the same place and still very naked.

She walks right up to me in her tight, black dress that hugs her hips so much, it makes my dick twitch. My eyes automatically roam her short, thick legs as she fumbles toward me, trying to get her heels back on. She slides her jacket on and stands directly in front of me. Her stature is tiny, but the death stare she displays makes her much bigger than she is. Her pretty, light brown eyes, the reason for my initial attraction to her, seem much darker now. So dark they almost appear black in this lighting. Or maybe she's just pissed.

This is not what I wanted.

I hate making women feel this way, especially her for some reason. This time, I'm having the urge to ask her to stay and watch a movie or something with me ... after I apologize, of course. By her look, I can tell it won't matter what I say right now. She's leaving. *For good*.

"One day, you'll meet a woman that will destroy you. I hope I'll get to see it." She smiles, rolling her eyes, and then leaves my hotel room and me standing there feeling like a dipshit. Before I know it, my feet are moving for the door, but as I open it, she's already on the elevator. I watch her stare angrily as the doors close on any idea I might've had for us.

It turns out she was right, however. It took less than a

year before I met that woman. The woman who ended up being the only person who could piss me off and make me laugh just like that. I'll never forget the day we met either, because I made a complete fool out of myself. The guy that usually made women fumble all over themselves was doing the fumbling.

# CHAPTER TWO

## At Least the Sauce is Good

I SIT BACK ON THE LONG BLACK LEATHER COUCH, twiddling my thumbs, wanting to waste as much time as possible in silence. I don't want to be here in this room being forced to talk about shit I otherwise would never spew. Not that I really am doing that right now.

I look around the home office of Roselyn West, studying her décor as I do every other morning I force myself to be here. Through the floor-to-ceiling double glass doors, I can see out to her manicured backyard with kids' toys scattered across the grass. Of course, my immediate thought is to the plans that were once made about my own family.

A family I never thought I wanted or deserved.

That dream has been stolen from me.

I finally look over to her as she folds her legs while sipping her coffee, I'm sure, hoping I pick today to finally speak. It's already been thirty minutes, and I can't get myself to say a word. But I definitely needed to be here. Unable to cope with such a loss, I decided to come to the one person who knew her the most. Us the most.

*Our therapist.*

I unwittingly pushed her to begin seeing West when I blew up on her a few months before her death. Eventually, she and I saw West as a couple to strengthen the trust in our relationship, but now I'm here alone. This was never supposed to be. I stare down at the engagement ring I placed on a necklace and wear beneath my shirt every day.

"Braxton, I know you're here for a reason. You need to talk to me at some point," she takes a deep sigh, "why not just tell me about the first time you met."

I smile happily, never missing the chance to share stories about my Phoenix. So I know she's doing this on purpose.

---

*It's a busy Saturday night dinner service at my restaurant, Braxton's on East. I'm usually frustrated during these services because shit always hits the fan. Not only that, but I have yet to learn you can't please everyone. Everyone's palettes are never the same.*

*Tonight, I don't want any complaints. An influential foodie is coming to feature my bistro, and I want everything to be perfect. I'll even accommodate special orders and substitutions, just to avoid any problems with the food.*

*The special of the day is Lamb Shank with a red wine sauce, which happens to be my favorite meal to make, and what the* foodie ordered. I've decided to bring the meal out to her myself and maybe even get a picture with her to up my followers. Something I only recently started paying attention to.

Because the restaurant is so busy, I turn slightly to avoid running into a customer with the foodie's meal. I suddenly spot a beautiful woman, sitting by herself, eating my Bouillabaisse, and reading a book. Her every move becomes personified, as my attention averts strictly to her. The bustling of the restaurant stills while I watch her subtly blow on the soup in her spoon, and then perch her lips to slowly suck the broth into her mouth.

She places the spoon in the bowl and slides her glasses back up her nose. I don't know what it is about her, but her simple beauty captures me, even though, from where I'm standing, I shouldn't have even seen her there.

The problem is, all this time I've been watching her, I've actually been moving forward. So much so that I end up bumping right into the foodie as she is live on social media. The entire plate of food falls directly on her head, and it's all caught on her Livestream.

I stand there in horror, not knowing what to do. The restaurant goes completely quiet as shocked onlookers point and stare at us. The foodie looks up at me, dumbfounded as the sauce drips down her Ravens ball cap, and chunks of the mashed potatoes fall on her lap. Luckily she's wearing jeans, so the hot food doesn't touch her bare skin.

To my surprise, she licks her lips and smiles into the camera. "Well, at least the sauce is good," she grabs a dinner napkin off of the table and wipes her phone screen quickly, "after I clean myself off here, Chef Braxton is going to try that again, and I'll be right back!"

She turns the broadcast off and places the phone on the table without even skipping a beat.

"I'm so sorry, Miss Bynum," I say, trying to wipe the mess surrounding her and picking up the plate that fell to the floor, while the busboy, Paolo, runs to assist.

"I think I may have some clothes in my car if you insist on staying," a woman says, but I only see her flat red shoes.

My eyes roam up quickly to the woman with the book. She smiles at me, but I don't move. I sit there like a buffoon, forgetting my words. Her bright, white teeth glimmer as her hazel eyes cause an uncontrollable rumbling within me, but I still can't budge. I'm in complete awe of a woman I don't even know. What the hell is wrong with me?

"That would be awesome ..." Bynum says, searching for a name.

"Phoenix," the beauty responds.

I finally realize I have legs and stand. I tower over her, which doesn't say much because I'm taller than most people at 6'3". She swipes the loose tendrils of her brownish-red hair behind her ear and pushes her glasses up again. I usually go for ladies that are much more provocatively dressed, makeup, and, well, desperate.

But there's nothing desperate about this one. She doesn't care what people think of her; she just does her own thing. And does it well. Even though she's just wearing jeans and a T-shirt, she's the sexiest woman I've ever seen in my life.

"You should probably get her meal ready," the woman I now know as Phoenix says, before leading Bynum out to her car.

I would never forget that night for many reasons. The main one being I made a total ass of myself live to Bynum's 500,000 followers, but also because I met her. Phoenix Brighton. The woman who saved my life that night and every day after for the next two years. But also the woman who flew away with my soul, destroying every ounce of who I thought I had become on the day of her death.

## CHAPTER THREE
### Fear

I look up to see West covering her mouth as if trying to contain her laughter. I admit, that night wasn't one of my finest moments and should have ended my career. Instead, it did the complete opposite.

"Oh, my God, just let the shit out already," I say, expecting the bellow that finally explodes from her mouth. She laughs so hard I join her glee.

*Laughter.*

Something I hadn't experienced for almost a year now. It became too much of a guilty pleasure. I never felt I deserved the slightest bit of happiness once she was gone. I suddenly catch myself in mid-chuckle, realizing what I have allowed myself to do and immediately become angry.

*I have to get out of here.*

I stand abruptly, wanting to jolt out of there before I say something mean and unwarranted.

"No! Sit! We still have fifteen minutes," West commands.

The tone in her voice convinces my body to return to its seated position without a fight. After all, this is the furthest she's gotten with me in six months, so I know she won't let me just walk out of here.

Well, I'm not really sure if the first five months counted, considering I canceled most of the sessions or left after just five minutes of sitting on this fucking couch. I couldn't bring myself to share the same seat Phoenix had once sat in.

West showed up at the only restaurant I have left and convinced me to talk right then and there, or I wouldn't be sitting here now. I respect her for getting me to release emotions I tried to bury. Granted, it began with anger and me punching a hole in my own restaurant's kitchen; nevertheless, it was the release I needed.

"I'm really not supposed to do this, but I feel you should know. It may help you. Have you heard the story of that night from her point of view?" West asks.

I stare at her, intrigued to finally hear why Phoenix disappeared that night and didn't return. She said she became too busy, but I knew there was more to it, especially after her death. Even now, her parents keep me in the dark and treat me as if none of this would have ever happened had I not pushed her to be with me.

"No. But I'd like to know," I admit.

She takes a deep breath, removing her notepad from her lap and placing it on the table beside her. She leans forward, laying her forearms on her thighs, and interlocks her fingers in front of her. "I had her keep a journal to make it easier for her to begin to express herself. This is what I learned from one of her entries."

---

*The day everything changed ...*

*I love it here. It's the only place I can find peace. Peace from life, my studies, my parents ... and my—forget it. I need to stop talking about that. What keeps me afraid and hidden. I never thought I would become this person. The person that hides from trouble, never being able to leave the house in fear something might happen. But once a month, on different days, I convinced myself to leave the house and find my place of solace. After all, it's been an entire year since I decided to try and distance myself from my responsibilities. I just should have never given in to my parents' plans for me. They have been controlling every ounce of my life since I was born.*

*But the day I went to design school is when I was able to cut the imaginary cord they had me tethered to. Now I was finally free to do as I pleased. Unfortunately, I did some things I wasn't proud of, including drinking far too much. So much so I somehow became addicted to it and was kicked out. I ended up right back in the clutches of my parents, who then tightened the cord they once loosened.*

*Unfortunately, that meant accelerating my father's plan for me.*

*That plan included marrying into a certain family to strengthen my father's already powerful name in the community.*

*The Brighton family is synonymous amongst the charity world in Potomac, and they refused to let their drunken daughter ruin it. They just didn't expect their plan to almost destroy it instead.*

*Nonetheless, on certain days, I am able to escape my family home and drive almost an hour away, just to feel safe. I read about the opening of Braxton's on East in Glenn Burnie, and I wish I could say it was the rave reviews that finally brought me here a few months ago. But it wasn't. It was the tall, handsome chef that graced the cover of the article that did it. His glistening muscular, chocolate skin awakened desires within me I forgot my body could produce. Obviously, I can't get involved with anyone, but it was something about his smile that made me want to meet him.*

*And I wasn't the only one apparently.*

*A month after the grand opening, I sat at the back of the restaurant, having a clear view of all the women that obviously thought the same thing. I've never seen so many women dressed so seductively in hopes of meeting the same man. A man that never came into the dining area of the restaurant.*

*But it turns out that didn't matter. Being a self-appointed epic food critic, I enjoyed every bite of the first meal I ordered. It had to be the best tasting short ribs I ever had in my young life. So, it ultimately became the food that brought me back. And every time, I wasn't disappointed. I was able to enjoy a quiet meal alone, safely, and not have to worry about being recognized in this part of Maryland. With no disruption of my serenity. My security.*

*Not until tonight anyway.*

*I'm here for the third time, completely enthralled with yet another meal and book, sitting in what has become my seating area. Being constantly terrified, I always need to sit in places closest to* an exit, but able to see my entire surroundings at all times. As I sip on Braxton's Bouillabaisse, I hear the loudest commotion coming from the middle of the restaurant.

I finally look up to see Chef Braxton has finally graced us with his presence, but clearly, he should never come out here. I watch him frantically try and clean off a young woman that's covered in his special of the day.

It's not until I recognize the young lady that I realize he's probably just made an earth-shattering mistake. I recognize Julia Bynum right away because I follow her reviews of restaurants all the time. She travels all around Maryland, finding all the hidden gems the state has to offer. I even find myself convincing my house manager to order me takeout just so I can try these foods during my daily picnics, that look so delicious on her live broadcasts. As good as the food looks, I'm never able to make it past the front porch on days other than my monthly visits here. Unless it's to my quiet place to eat lunch on my parents' massive property.

I stare at the situation, wanting to help the guy out, more so because I don't want her to destroy his reputation, therefore ruining my monthly getaway. I remember I always have clothes in the car, mainly outfits I've designed myself, but I'm sure there's something I can offer her. Although, when I approach him, he still seems dumbstruck and unable to move. So I try to nudge him on as I grab Julia and take her to my car.

Without a second thought, I walk outside and straight for my car, not even looking around first. Something I've had to do regardless of where I am. Even going into my own bedroom. I've just never felt secure in my surroundings ... my home ... my skin.

As we get closer to my car, I pull out the fob to pop the trunk, revealing all of the clothes I've designed and never made it to a boutique, only to the trunk.

"Oh. My. God." She pulls out the black and red striped romper I had just added to my not-going-anywhere collection. "This is so cuuuttte! Can I wear this?" She eyes me awestruck, as if she's just won the lottery, but really it's a no-name design, sewn by a nobody.

"Sure. Have at it," I say, waving my hands at her and unzipping my get-out-of-dodge bag. I move around the extra sets of clothes and toiletries to find the washrag and towel I always have in there. After finding the matching set, I hand it to her. "You can never be too prepared," I say as she gives me the same look everyone else gives me at some time or another. Confusion and concern.

She saunters away from me to clean up in the bathroom, I'm sure, but turns suddenly as we hit the foyer of the restaurant. "Who shall I credit for such generosity ... and who made this?" She tries to find the tag, which only reads PB Designs because I haven't thought of a name yet.

"I did. Phoenix Brighton, and I also made that—" I stop abruptly, realizing what I've just done. I have to get the fuck out of here.

Before she stops me, I run straight to my car to get the hell out of here. I can't believe I erased these past two years of being extra careful, just like that! I can never come back here now. Great!

---

I sit there with many questions swirling in my head. First, of course, I wonder why I hadn't noticed her before that night. But as she used to remind me constantly, everything happens for a reason. I stare at the clock, realizing our time is up and probably only have time to ask her one question.

"Why would Bynum mentioning her by name keep her from coming to my restaurant? Why was she so afraid?"

"You really don't know?"

I shake my head in response.

"Braxton, Phoenix was being stalked."

## CHAPTER FOUR

### Back to Basics

WHAT THE HELL AM I SUPPOSED TO DO WITH THAT? I probably shouldn't be pissed, but I'm fucking fuming. I begged her to be honest with me—tell me what she was keeping from me—but she insisted it was all in my head. But when you grow to love someone, you can tell when they're keeping something from you. I don't understand why she couldn't trust me enough to just tell me. I could have protected her. Instead, now she's fucking dead.

I stride down the street, angrily approaching Braxton's on East, the last restaurant I now have after the disaster of the past year. The one refuge I've always had was cooking, but now I can't seem to find the right recipe or come up with anything new and exciting anymore. I lost my ambition, and in turn, lost two restaurants.

As I approach the door, I see my manager quickly walking toward me in her annoyingly loud heels, but I just hold my hand up to stop whatever bullshit she wants to talk about. Her entire body sinks in defeat as I barge into the kitchen.

"Get out!" I shout at the line as they prep for tonight's same old menu.

They scurry from the kitchen without a second thought, and I find myself alone in what used to be my sanctuary. My solemn place. The calming sounds of the bubbling water from the pots left on the stove, the steam and smells of fresh truffles fill the air, but all I can remember is her laughter echoing from the walls. I tried to teach her to cook in this very kitchen. Before I know it, I'm tossing a full pot of steaming hot water to the floor, tossing all the hard work the line accomplished this morning across the room, grabbing everything I find, from vegetables to utensils, and throwing them at whatever wall I aim toward. Unfortunately, my manager, Reyna, walks into the kitchen just as I toss a plate at the door. Luckily for me and my pockets, she ducks.

"Reyna!" I charge for her as she timidly stands, making sure no shards of glass have ended up in her short, quaffed hair. I grab her hands, helping her to stand before checking her bare arms and face for any cuts.

"Mr. Knight, I'm fine."

"Why are you in here?" I grunt.

She stares at the mess I've made, no doubt wondering how we will possibly be ready for dinner service tonight.

"I thought you should see this," she says, handing me her tablet.

I reluctantly grab it from her, knowing whatever she

needs to show me must be important enough for her to come in here during one of my tantrums. It's a wonder why anyone wants to work for me anymore.

I hit play on what looks like a video, and it's a familiar face. Julia Bynum.

*"Hey, peeps! I've decided it's time to revisit certain restaurants. Oh, you know the ones. Those delicious eateries I totally made famous. What can I say? I'm quite the foodie that just happens to be a cutie with a ton of even cuter followers. So what do you say? Pop in the comments and tell me which places I should surprise within the next few weeks. I'll only choose five. Laters!"*

My eyes widen, hoping my name isn't mentioned in the comments. I scroll down only to find that not only was I mentioned, but I also got the top vote!

"Fuck, no!" I shout, shoving the tablet back into Reyna's hands, then turn to clean this massive mess I've made.

"Oh c'mon, Mr. Knight, we need this. If you haven't noticed, you haven't exactly been filling up the seats every night of the week like you used to." She stumbles, trying to keep up with me.

"You think I don't know that!" I snap, suddenly stopping in front of her, causing her to knock into me. I turn away and continue to clean. "I just don't want that type of publicity right now."

She stops following me, crosses her arms, and taps her foot on the floor. I know that tap all too well. Phoenix used to do that shit when she was about to tell me off.

"Well, I'm glad you're finally thinking of someone other

than yourself, Braxton Knight. I mean, obviously, you're the end-all-be-all, and we're here to serve you. We couldn't possibly still be here working for an emotional, uncontrollable tyrant for the hell of it." She takes a step forward. "No, we don't have families to feed, people to take care of, and bills to pay. We're here for the fun of it. Thank you for finally thinking of the rest of us!"

*Asshole*, she whispers under her breath. She turns on her heels and walks out swiftly, leaving me with her tirade.

Yes, I'm such a fucking asshole. I stare at the room I destroyed, disregarding the work my people came in early to complete. I have to fix this. Earn their respect again, if that is even possible at this point.

I slowly put the kitchen back together, thinking about the homework West sent me away with today. I normally just ignore her requests, but this time, I feel it's best for me to stop being selfish and try to get back to me. I have a team to look after, which depends on my leadership. So today, I'll do what she asked.

Even though it seemed absolutely impossible at the time. So much so, she wrote it on the back of her business card so I can't act like it was never said. I pull the card from my pocket and flip it over to her note:

**Think of only cooking for one hour. Create something new.**

*I can do this.*

For one hour, I will try not to think of what I've lost, rather what I still have. But first thing's first. I gather myself before walking out into the dining area and facing the people I've obviously disappointed the most. I immediately hear the hushed sniffles of Reyna, who is being consoled by my sous chef, Mason. She has been invaluable to my brand since this place took off, so she definitely does not deserve to be treated this way, and neither does he.

*Mason.* I owe him a drink. He's been carrying this restaurant with what little I've been able to teach him over the years. Although he's only four years younger than me at twenty-three, he reminds me of myself.

"He's going to fire me," Reyna whispers, muffled into Mason's chest.

"I wouldn't dare. I need you here to keep me in check, obviously." I smile as she turns quickly to face me then stands, shoving away from Mason quickly. *Hmmm, that was awkward.*

"Mr. Knight, I'm so sor—" Reyna starts.

"Don't. You're fine." I walk forward to take her hand into mine and keep her at my side as I address the staff, who are all eyeing me cautiously. "Okay, so I've basically been told by this young lady that I've been selfish this past year. I could make excuses because of my loss, but I'm not." I put my head down, trying to block out the impending barrage of memories I'm currently trying to suppress.

Reyna squeezes my hand for assurance, and then it finally hits me at that moment for some reason. It could be the single tear that has fallen down her cheek or the solemn looks on my staff's faces that reminds me we've all lost her in some way. Phoenix was a fixture here in the last month of her life, and friends to all of these people, especially Reyna and Mason.

Mason stands suddenly. "Honestly, man, she's the reason we're all still here. We knew you needed time. But..." He comes over to stand on the other side of me and drapes his long arms across my shoulder. "I think it's time, man. To get back to the place she loved. You know?"

I do know.

He's absolutely right. She would be ashamed of how I let this place go downhill. I look around the room as the rest of the staff stand in solidarity, knowing these people before me are more than just my staff. They're my people. My friends. And it's time I treat them as such. "You heard him. Let's put this place back on the map! We need to be prepared for Bynum's visit next month."

With that, everyone scurries, and I can't think of anything else I'd rather be doing right now. Cooking.

## CHAPTER FIVE

### Stupid Look

"Try this!" I excitedly barge into my session with West, wanting her to try one of the signature dishes I've been serving. Since I did what she suggested after our last appointment, cooking has become my main focus again. "You have to eat it now while it's still hot." I place the container on her desk as she beams with excitement, mirroring my own expression.

"So, you actually did what I asked this time?" she questions as she removes the clear lid and smells the aromas that escape almost immediately. "Smells delicious, Braxton."

"It's crab cakes with confit fingerlings, asparagus, and a little tarragon tartar on the side. It's been doing well in the restaurant, but I'm not sure I want this to be the dish for our visit with Bynum." I plop down on the sofa, not even thinking about staying on my side of the couch. Something

I always did as if the ghost of Phoenix literally sits beside me.

I lie back, place my feet up on the couch, and interlock my hands on my stomach. My mind has been trying to come up with the perfect recipe, something different. But nothing.

"Well, Braxton, first, this is absolutely delicious. I wasn't even hungry, and now I've eaten the entire thing." She giggles as I proudly peek over at her pretty much empty container. "Second," she giggles again, "you're about to have another visit from Julia Bynum?"

I chuckle. "Why is that funny?"

She stares at me with that you-know-why look. "Although that live stream went viral and skyrocketed your restaurants, it was a disaster!" She grabs her notepad and pen before she sits in the usual chair opposite the couch. "So, clearly, you're in a better mood today. Not that I'm complaining, but what brought this on?" She sits back, crossing her leg, and readies her pen to take notes.

I sit up quickly, leaning forward and placing my elbows on my thigh. I look over to the right, imagining Phoenix smiling beside me as she sits Indian style with her shoes off. I never understood how she felt so comfortable in these types of situations, but she had no qualms about sharing when we were here. I just wish we had more time for her to share the important things she purposely left out.

It's as if she trusted West and this space but to a point. I stare at her, wondering what happened to make Phoenix trust her so willingly. Whatever it was, I'd like for her to tell me. I'm sure she's not supposed to, but she did tell me more than I already knew. And although I'm in better moods these days, we still need to talk about that bomb she dropped at the end of our last session.

"I did what you asked," I stand abruptly and walk over to her floor-to-ceiling, French glass doors that overlook her backyard. "I have questions about Phoenix and this stalker I should've had the chance to shoot!" My mood quickly turns to anger as I ball my fist at my sides, coping with the fact that she basically lied to me our entire relationship. Come to think of it, this could have been why her parents were so protective over her. Why they tried to keep us apart.

"I've already told you more than you need to know. Granted, that may have been a mistake, but I knew it would be the only way you'd finally open up."

"And it worked," I turn around to face her, "see, I'm even smiling." I produce a fake smile to her amusement.

"That may be so, but the things she told me were in confidence."

I sit in front of her calmly, prepared to beg if needed. I know for certain learning the truth about her, or as much as I can anyway, will help me to move on. Moving on is something I need to do, or I will lose the last thing I have left. My restaurant. So, in order for me to get what I want, I'll just have to bribe West. Although she's smart enough to know that's what I'm doing, she'll go with it. In the end, we both want the same thing.

"I have a proposition for you," I initiate, sitting up further to the edge of the couch.

"Why don't I like the sound of this?" She puts the pen and pad down on the table beside her.

"C'mon, hear me out first." I smile flirtatiously as I used to, before Phoenix, when I wanted to get my way with women. Something I know West will never fall for, but I can't resist the temptation.

"Phoenix told me about this stupid look you get on your face when you want something." She giggles, and I find myself laughing along with her even though it was at my expense. Turns out, I do remember how to have a sense of humor.

"Alright, alright, I'm sorry." I put my hands up in submission. "Look, I'll stop fighting this process of yours if you're willing to share one thing I don't know about Phoenix with each visit."

She sits back in the chair and stares silently for far too long before finally saying anything. "Braxton, the only way I will agree to do this is if we talk about that night."

"West, I—" I start.

She puts her hand up. "Not today. I will give you a few more sessions. That's a few weeks since my vacation is coming, but some things you don't know. Take it or leave it."

I lean my back against the back of the couch, my body slumped in defeat while I realize I have no choice in the matter. Taking a look to the right, I imagine Phoenix's smile of encouragement—a smile I know all too well.

If I agree to this, I will have to talk about the day I lost her. The night I was going to ask her to be my wife but found her unconscious body instead. The day I thought my life ended. But here I am, still waking up each morning, taking breaths I shouldn't be allowed to, but not finding the strength to live each day as if it were the last.

"When do we start?"

"Well, you're here now. So, let's talk about your first date."

"Why? You know that story well." I sit up, somewhat annoyed, knowing if I go down this road, I will possibly run out of here pissed again.

"I do. But I want you to tell me again in as much detail as possible." She smiles, picking up that annoying-ass pad and pen as if she's about to write something new.

"Fine."

## CHAPTER SIX

### Now You May Go

ONE YEAR AGO ...

That was so fucking embarrassing. I can't believe I tossed an entire plate of food on Julia Bynum during a Livestream! I sit quietly and alone, stewing in my own screw-ups, constantly rewinding the dumbass look on my face as she swipes the gravy from her eyes. Each time I replay it, the watch count goes up by the thousands, pissing me off even further. This was supposed to be my big break finally. The youngest black chef in Maryland to own their very own franchise, but now I've certainly ruined it.

Oh, my God! I'm such a fucking idiot!

And, of course, it was done in front of her. I could probably blame this on her anyway because she totally distracted me. After this, I doubt she'll even come back. I'm sure it was Phoenix's first time; there's no way I would have missed her before. Or maybe. I've never really needed to go out into the dining area until I'm done cooking.

"Don't beat yourself up, Mr. Knight. I'm sure it will all work out," Mason, one of the line cooks I hired when I opened, walks back into the kitchen.

"Ha! I don't know about that."

He pulls his jacket on as he's about to leave. "Well, I do, sir. Besides, in the end, she loved your food." He smiles and leaves just as quickly as he came in. I hate it that he calls me sir here because we're actually friends now. But he insists on keeping it professional in the kitchen.

However, he's right about one thing. Bynum was gracious enough to let me have a redo, and she raved about the food ... and her clothes! I pick my tablet back up to let the video play through to the end, where she talks about the woman who gave her an outfit.

**"So, not only did I get the best lamb dinner ever, I got this cool new outfit. Tell me what you think so I can give props to the designer, Phoenix Brighton!"**

"That's it! That's her name!" I shout far too loudly.

But what should I do about it? I can't just start looking for her like some damn psycho. I'll just have to wait in hopes she'll come back here. Which I honestly doubt considering she ran out of here so fast tonight, she left without paying.

I was going to comp her meal anyway, but I'd like to know if she's that type who enjoys a meal and then finds a way to leave without paying. I mean, shit, I have done it myself once or twice.

There's not much I can do about it tonight anyway, so I put the ruining-my-life video away and go home.

The next morning, I learn just how powerful the Internet really is. As I do every morning, I'm brushing my teeth with the local news blaring as if I'm going deaf when I hear the anchor mention my restaurant's name. I run out of the bathroom with foamy toothpaste pouring from my mouth to see what's happening.

I can't contain my excitement as I turn up the volume even further. Even though I see the headline for the video is Fumble of the Day, and they're all laughing uncontrollably as if they aren't professionals, it doesn't matter.

I'm on the fucking news!

I jump up and down in place as if my favorite basketball team just won the championship, totally forgetting I have a mouth full of toothpaste oozing out of my mouth and to the floor. My neighbors are going to think I've lost my mind at 5:30 in the morning.

I run into the bathroom to rinse my mouth out and grab a towel to wipe up my mess before taking my chances and flipping through other channels to see if I'm mentioned. Not seeing anything, I jump on the computer to check my social media to see what's trending. All I see are notifications and direct messages.

"I'm trending! I'm-fuckin'-trending!" I shout just as my phone rings. I answer immediately, seeing it's Mason.

"Bruh! Are you seeing this shit?" he asks, not even waiting for me to answer, knowing I would be up because we always work out together on Monday mornings.

"I know! If I would've thought spilling food on a critic would do this, I would have done it opening day!" We both laugh.

"I told you it would all work out."

"You did. Too bad it's Monday, and we're closed! We need to build on this momentum," I regret that decision immediately.

"True, but if you hire one of those people who take care of these situations, you can still build on this."

"You know what?" I scroll through the direct messages,

*avoiding the ones asking for dates or telling me how sexy I am, straight to the one I noticed right away. The one whose profile photo was completely professional. "I got a message from this lady who says she's a Brand Ambassador. I'll message her."*

*"Listen to you. You big-time now, my dude."*

*We both laugh. "Don't worry; I'll be right here to keep your head out the clouds."*

*My mind shifts simultaneously to the person I feel helped me get the second chance. If it weren't for her, I would have just sat there like some idiot. Now, I really have to find her. "Dude, that chick from last night that got Bynum a change of clothes, have you seen her at the restaurant?"*

*"The bookworm? Yeah, she's been there a few times."*

*The bookworm.*

*Mason has a name for every regular that comes to my restaurant. It's his way of remembering them and their preferences, which make me want to train him to be my sous chef. His eye for detail and keeping the customers happy, even though that's not his job right now, is impeccable.*

*"Speaking of, she called right when Reyna closed up. She didn't pay or something. I don't know, anyway, Rey had already closed up the system, so she took down her information and said she would process the payment on Tuesday."*

*Her information!*

*That's fucking perfect. I could possibly pay a visit to her house and make up some stupid excuse about the bill. That's not too stalker-ish. Maybe a little, but I have a few hours to try and come up with something. Wait a minute.*

"How do you know about this? Since when do you and Reyna—wait, I mean," I clear my throat, "Rey, get so close?" I chuckle.

"Shut the hell up, bruh. It's not like that. We're just hanging out a bit."

"Umm-hmm, I bet you are." I laugh out loud.

"Whatevs! You coming to the gym or not?"

"I'll be there. One."

"One."

I fall back on the bed, letting it all sink in. I know everything is going to happen so fast from this point on. I want to build on this momentum, maybe even open up a third restaurant in my hometown.

Either way, I need to contact the brand ambassador to see if she can help me. I don't know shit about no social media. If it weren't for Reyna, I wouldn't have it, nor would I have anything on it. On second thought, maybe Reyna can help me build on this. She's the one who got Julia Bynum to come to the restaurant in the first place.

Reyna. I shoot her a text first to see if she could tell me where she wrote Phoenix's information down because I plan to pay her a visit this evening. There's no way I'm going another day without at least being able to thank her for her assistance.

Although, I know my intentions will wander further than that. I'm not sure why I'm so curious about this woman, but I'm willing to explore those reasons. I'm tired of being a bachelor. I've already lost the opportunity to get to know many good women. I'm not losing this one too.

*It seemed like I rushed through the workout today. Something I wouldn't usually do or allow whoever is working out with me to do. I try to take care of my body as much as I can because of all the fatty foods I have to make, and therefore, love to taste.*

*That has nothing to do with my taste in women, however. The ladies I'm interested in are as curvy as possible and filled out in all the right places. I have no interest in women who are typically in here and flirting with me. The ones I feel I will break in half.*

*I instantly think of Phoenix, and my dick twitches. She may have had on clothes that hid her body, but I can tell what's under there—and craving to see more. Unfortunately for Mason, my urge surpasses the need to workout. I gather my things quickly, hoping he doesn't give me too much of a hard time.*

"Yo, that's it? It's only been an hour," Mason says, grabbing his towel to wipe the sweat from his head and neck.

*I stare at him, knowing I must look as bad as he does. So I take a whiff of my funky underarms and double-time it so I can take an extensive shower. I'm already going to show up at her place uninvited ... I don't want to stink while I'm doing it.*

"I have to take care of something," I say, rushing toward the door as he extends his arms out in confusion. "I'll call you later."

*I waste no time taking a shower and giving myself a shape-up before heading to the restaurant to find her address, which Reyna placed in the safe I keep locked in my desk.*

*Once I see that she lives in Potomac, however, I become a little discouraged. Clearly, she's out of my league if she can afford to live there. She can't be that much older than me.*

*I plop in my black leather office chair, deciding if I should even waste my time. But the image of her reading her book, sitting at* the back of my restaurant, and then going out of her way to help me doesn't suggest she's a snob by any means.

So, I shake off the insecurities and head for my truck. After all, I may not have the money she has now, but I'm no fucking slouch. I'll get there and very soon. I start my Cayenne, let the engine roar as I tap on the gas like a big-ass kid. I've always loved the sound of these cars since I was a kid, and I had to own one. I pull off quickly, realizing I have a forty-five-minute drive ahead of me.

Once the flag appears on my navigation, I know I'm in the vicinity of her home. The large properties only make me want to work harder and own something like this one day. I turn down a dead-end block that shows only trees and open land at first.

Eventually, at the end of the cul-de-sac, a large, tall mansion appears. It's a beautiful home, but it has indescribable darkness to it. A darkness I wouldn't usually approach if I weren't dead set on talking to the owner. It's not gated, which is unusual to me, but I do see the abundance of video cameras immediately. I drive a little further, onto the stone driveway and around the large fountain in the middle to park in front of the ghostly home.

I, of course, hesitate once again, thinking this may not be the best of ideas, but I've come all this way already. I step out of my car, adjusting my sweatpants and tank top that I instantly regret wearing here, then walk timidly to the front door. As I approach, I glance up to the top of the home and spot a woman with what seems to be very long, dark-colored hair staring down at me. I can't make out her face, but she disappears so fast I wouldn't have been able to if I tried.

As I reach the top step and attempt to knock on the door, it swings open, and a large, intense man in a suit with a long ponytail *appears. He looks me up and down in somewhat disgust before crossing his hands in front of him.*

"Can I help you?" he asks.

"I guess. My name is Braxton Knight, here to see Phoenix Brighton."

*He chuckles at first, but clears his throat, recognizing his rude outburst only to continue with the same attitude.* "I'm sorry, sir, but she's not expecting visitors at the moment. Try again, never."

*What the fuck?*

*I ball my fist at the utter disrespect, but anger won't make a good impression. It doesn't matter anyway because he steps back and slams the door in my face just as quickly as he opened it.*

*Son of a bitch!*

*Clearly, this woman has more layers to her than meets the eye. The fact that I was just disrespected by some giant in a suit makes me want to know her that much more. I should have texted her anyway. Or even called. Something I rarely do these days unless I'm calling my parents.*

*I step back from the front door just enough to peek up to the window where I saw the figure looming, but the woman's gone. I'm sure that was her, so she knows I'm here. If she wanted to see me, she would've come down. Still, I pull out my phone and scroll through my contacts to Phoenix's now stored info.*

**I would like to speak with you in person. Call me. Braxton Knight.**

*I jog to my car, staring at my phone as I get in. I sit there motionless, staring at the screen, hoping she'll respond. Nothing. This may have been a total waste of time, but at least she knows my intentions ... for the most part, anyway.*

*I start my car without revving the engine this time and drive around her circular driveway and out of view from her large home and sight of the cameras. I just can't see where they would put them along these dense trees.*

*If I lived in this area, I would cut all this shit down. As I admire the quaintness of the view, I lose focus of the road in front of me, knowing there are no houses in this part of the dead end. I just didn't expect someone to dart out into the street. I slam on the brakes as hard as I can to avoid hitting her. As soon as the truck stops, I jump out of the car and run to her, pulling her into my arms.*

*"Are you fucking crazy?!" I shout, holding her at arm's length. I glance over the area, figuring out where she could have come from.*

*She giggles. "You said you needed to speak to me."*

*I eye her curiously, first wondering why I feel like she needed to sneak out to see me, and second, why does she have to be so damn beautiful. She stands quietly in front of me in her pinkish summer dress, hair out and flowing, bare skin with no makeup ... just flawless.*

*It's hard for me to maintain focus with her wide hazel eyes blinking rapidly up at me, her long lashes accentuating her beauty. Her hair blows in the wind as it swirls below her butt. It was in a bun the last time I saw it, and I didn't realize how long it was.*

*She smiles wider as I'm sure she notices how floored I am. She's captivated me so easily. My eyes finally meet those thin, soft lips of hers, and I have to beg my impulses to behave. I've already had her in my grasps for far too long. I release her quickly and restore some sort of dignity.*

*"Yes, I wanted to thank you for your help yesterday. Your meal*

will, of course, be comp'd." I smile, placing my hands in the pockets of my sweatpants.

Oh God, I totally wore the wrong shit today. I adjust the growing bulge in my pants without her noticing.

"Oh, I couldn't ask you to do that. However, I am a little peeved that your manager shared my personal information after I explicitly implored her not to," she says, annoyed, furrowing her brow.

I chuckle to myself, wondering if this is supposed to be her pissed-off face. If that's the case, I'll never take her seriously.

How am I planning our future already?

"I am the boss, so I wouldn't be too upset with her. Also, I insist you let me do this for you."

She thinks about it for a minute and accepts my offer. "Fine, but I would like you to have lunch with me. Do you have time?"

"For you, I'll make time stand still." I smile, embarrassed that I said something so fucking cheesy, but honest. I am pleased to see her blush as a result.

"You can leave your car here. No one's coming through here for a while," she says, turning away, and I follow at her heels. "You should turn your car off." She gestures to my running truck.

What the fuck is wrong with me?

Why am I letting her get to me like this? I jog around to the driver's side, turn off the engine, and grab my phone before joining her again. I follow her through the dense, large trees until there's suddenly an opening into a well-manicured valley surrounded by colorful flowers. A much brighter, welcoming area than that of her home. She walks over to where she has a basket and blanket waiting.

"Do you always picnic alone?" I ask as I grab the blanket from her hands and spread it on the grass. This isn't something I would usually like, but I'm still shocked she hasn't yelled at me for showing up unannounced. But she doesn't seem like the type that would do too much yelling.

"It's the only time I'm able to be completely alone with my own thoughts. No one knows about this particular spot on the property, considering my parents are often away on business."

So, she lives with her parents. We sit on the blanket as she pulls out a lot of food from the basket. My eyes widen at the variety she's eating at one time.

"You eat all of this for lunch?" I stare at her and wonder why she isn't bigger than she is.

She laughs out, throwing her head back as she does. I don't know what it is about that sound, but I hope I hear it much more in the future.

"Don't be ridiculous. I knew my father's goon would send you off when I saw you get out of the car from my window."

"So, that was you," I insinuate as she hands me a plate, and I start to pick at the fruit.

She nods. "Yeah, so I just went about my day packing my lunch in the kitchen when I got your text."

I grab one of the sandwiches, snatching it from the bag and biting into it, not realizing how hungry I am. "You mean the text you never responded to? That one?" I joke.

She laughs. "I was too busy packing all this. I'm just glad I was able to beat you down the road. I had to take a shortcut."

"Of course."

We spend the next hour talking. She quickly dodges each and

every question I ask about her family and why her home is so protected, but that doesn't keep me from craving more. I want her to tell me everything she is willing to share in the time I have her.

She does tell me her father is Native American, which is why she isn't allowed to cut her hair. As she put it, the only time she is allowed to is in mourning.

However, I don't hold back from her. I feel the need to share hidden feelings that I've suppressed for many years. Why I refused relationships and just kept my mind focused on my dreams. Dreams that, thanks to her, I am able to propel with her one simple gesture. I feel indebted to her. And the more she laughs and smiles at me, the more I don't want this moment to end.

She checks the time on her smartwatch and quickly begins to gather everything and toss it in the basket.

"Let me help you," I offer. I end up grabbing for the same fork as her, and our hands touch.

We sit there motionless as we let the butterflies flow between us without a word. The sound of the wind flowing through the grass and flowers, along with the pounding of my chest, are the only things I hear. I want to ask her for more time, but I know the answer, and I don't want to press her any further. I want her to know I'm here and willing to listen. I look up at her, but she keeps her eyes fixated on our hands. The urge to feel the smoothness of her lips is overwhelming, but I slowly lean forward and settle for a soft peck against her forehead.

"C'mon, let's get this cleaned up."

She finally looks at me and smiles as we gather everything up quickly before she shows me the way out of this maze, to my car. The sun is starting to set as we finally get to my Cayenne, and I'm *pretty ecstatic. I spent more time with her than I anticipated. She wasn't as pissed as I thought she would be.*

*Could it be possible she noticed me before? I immediately thought of the feature a local food blog did on me around the time we opened. I can't even front, I know a lot of women frequented the restaurant from that point on because they wanted a chance to meet me, and I'm sure it wasn't to taste my barbecue. However, she seems far from the type that would throw herself at any man, for any reason.*

"Can I ask you a question?"

"Ugh! More questions?" She giggles.

*I grab her hand as we get to the passenger side of my truck. The look of shock crosses her face as she stares at our connection but doesn't pull away. Instead, she interlocks her tiny fingers with mine.*

"Why did you come to my restaurant ... initially?" *I immediately feel her body tense. I can tell she's about to run or at least try to, so I know she started to come for me but is too shy to admit it.* "Can I see you again?"

*She contemplates the thought, staring down the road toward her home and then in the opposite direction. She glares down at the ground.* "I just don't see how that's possible."

*I want to implore her to tell me why she thinks she's trapped, but I know she won't. Regardless, for now, I'll take what I can get.* "Can I join you for lunch next week? Same time?"

*She looks up at me, confused, but then smiles, letting me know she is fine with it.* "Okay. I'd like that."

*I stare at her lips for far too long as I bite on my lower lip, trying to evade my impulses, wanting to do what I shouldn't.* "So, I'll text you later?"

She smiles. "I look forward to it. Talk to you later then." *She pulls her hand from mine and turns away from me quickly to get back in her house, I'm sure.*

*But I can't let her go for some reason. My own need and desires that I've kept cornered all day have come out, forcing my legs forward enough to grab at her arm and pull her back to me. I spin her quickly and back her into my truck. My body towers over her as I lean my right arm above her head onto the hood of the Cayenne. She doesn't stop me or push me away, her eyes down, not daring to look up at me. I place my left palm on her cheek, lifting her head up to face me. She glares through me, her greenish-brown eyes to my dark brown. I feel her body begin to tremble, and her breathing intensifies.*

"Not so fast," *I whisper. I let my right hand glide from her cheek to the nape of her neck and quickly bend down to kiss her. The initial touch is slow and intentional as our lips find their rhythm. Their own connection. They slowly part and then back together, pressing more firmly against each other. The smoothness of her lips feels gratifying as I scantily pull her bottom lip into my mouth. She slowly wraps her arms around my waist, subtly letting her hands roam my back. The touch of her hands against the thin material of my tank only makes me smother her lips harder, shoving my tongue in her mouth. She reciprocates with the same ardor, but keeping our same rhythm.*

*I've never kissed anyone like this. So deliberate and steady. Although I've never let anyone get this close to me, there's only one other woman that I considered the possibility with. I screwed that shit up. Not this time. I've decided to open myself up to Phoenix. From this moment on, I wouldn't want to feel this with anyone else.*

*I slowly pull away from her, placing my forehead on hers. The trembling has subsided, and her breaths are less labored.*

"Now, you may go." *I chuckle.*

"Well, thank you for the permission." *She giggles as I give her the space to walk away from me. I watch her as she disappears back into the woods, and I have this overwhelming feeling everything is about to change.*

# CHAPTER SEVEN

## Homework

"And it did. For the better, for a while," I admit.

"Things are still for the better. Even though you've suffered a great loss, you're learning to overcome it. That's what's important," she reassures.

I sigh. "Am I, though? It took you telling me something I should've known from Phoenix herself to get me to even talk." I shake my head and let it drop down, facing the floor. "She didn't trust me enough to tell me that after a year of keeping shit a secret. I'm such a fucking idiot!" I shout, standing abruptly. The anger finds its way back out of me, and I feel like I'm about to lose it again. "She had me feeling for her, following behind her like some goddamn puppy, had me thinking it was her parents ... and it was someone out there I could have just protected her from." I fight back the tears that well in my eyes as I become more and more infuriated.

I think back to the final month of our relationship

when she finally told her family about us. I also think about her insisting we stay indoors. Everything becomes so much clearer now.

"Her parents, well, father, were part of the problem because they knew who was stalking her."

I turn swiftly to face her, instantly even more pissed because I don't know any father who would allow some man to bring harm to his daughter. At least that's what he said to me when he surprised me at my restaurant once she came clean to him.

"They had no idea how bad things had become. Part of that was Phoenix's responsibility," she finishes.

Curiosity brings me back to the couch. I sit there silently waiting for the next blow to my mind. I hope I'll be able to stay calm enough to not destroy my kitchen this time.

"Things started out innocently, and Phoenix had confined herself with the idea of—" she hesitates, pissing me off further. "...An arranged marriage, in a sense."

My mind goes blank momentarily as her words continue to echo in my head like some dumbass song that keeps playing on the radio.

"I'm sorry ... what the fuck did you just say?"

"Braxton ..."

"No! Repeat it!"

"She was promised to another man, Braxton. It was to further her family's name and their position."

I stand, ignoring that last part of her statement, as my heart begins to pang violently through my chest. "She was engaged? And fucking me?" I step away from her, then stop suddenly. "She was engaged to another man," I clarify as if I might have misheard her.

"In a way, yes. But he started to become possessive over her. She felt her freedom and safety slipping away, especially after the first time he hit her ... then eventually tried to kill her."

"What! He hit her? Tried to kill her! Who is this mother fucker?"

"Braxton, you can't avenge her. So, is that really important now?"

"Yes!"

"Sit down."

"I'm not sitting anywhere. Tell me who it was because there's a bullet with his name on it."

"Braxton, sit!" she shouts.

I pout, not wanting to give in to her demand. But the look in her eyes urges me to do as she says. I try to calm down, not wanting to take twenty steps back. But the more that is revealed to me, the more I want to kill somebody.

"Listen, she didn't want to be engaged to the guy ... she was being forced. She knew the only way she'd guarantee more time was to persuade her father into thinking she's not ready to be a wife. Regardless of his status, he loved his daughter. So much so that she knew if he had knowledge of the truth, he would kill this guy. That wouldn't be good for either family."

There's obviously more to this family than I anticipated. But I have a feeling asking about it won't get me any answers right now.

"Phoenix also didn't want her father to think she was a failure," she adds.

"That is absolutely ridiculous. Not only that, but they should have known something was off. To go from accepting the marriage to not at the snap of a finger ..." I hang my head, "...but I should have known too. I guess."

"Don't do it. We're moving forward. It's time for your homework."

"I'm not in the mood." I fall back against the couch, feeling defeated.

"Unfortunately, our agreement doesn't depend on your mood."

I throw my hands up. "Fine. What are you torturing me with now?"

"Well, you and Mason are pretty good friends now, correct?"

I sit up, wondering where she's going with this. "We are."

"I think it's time for you to be a friend again. Why not have a guys' night out? Tonight."

"Tonight?"

"Yes. Time's up. I expect to hear about it when you're back." She stands, not giving me time to fight her on this. She knows damn well I wouldn't go out now. I just don't see the point. *God, I hope he's too busy.*

"Fine. I'll see you Wednesday." I slowly saunter out of her home office and to my truck parked directly in front of her house. I pull out my phone, hoping he doesn't want to go out so I can go home to nothing but my thoughts of Phoenix and her lies.

I just can't believe she's a fucking liar. I told her everything possible about me, hoping that she would just tell me everything. Instead, she just says it's her father that's keeping us apart to placate me. After all, I know how some people with money are. I assumed it was because her family thought less of me since I wasn't as established. I made a complete ass of myself.

I scroll through the contacts of my phone and settle on a text to Mason. If he doesn't respond by the time I get home, I'm staying in.

***I feel like hitting up Chasers tonight. You in?***

I put the phone in the cup holder and start my car. Before I can put it in gear, the car tells me I've received a text message.

***I'm in. See you at ten.***

Well, there goes my plan to wallow in my own misery.

# CHAPTER EIGHT

## Best of Terms

When I pull up to the lounge, it's completely crowded. Why there are so many people out on a Monday night, I have no idea, but I want absolutely no part of it. I press my foot on the brake, tempted to push the start button, but I remember Mason is expecting me, and it would be rude of me not to go in. Fuck it.

I hop out of the truck and approach the back of the line in search of Mason, but he's nowhere in sight. Great!

"Braxton Knight, if you don't get over here, honey," a familiar voice grabs my attention to the front of the line.

I look behind me and see the door girl waving me back up. This used to be my hangout before Phoenix. I didn't expect the same girl to be here.

"Veronica, what are you still doing here?" I ask as she pulls me into a tight hug. She's always been very grabby. She still wears entirely too much makeup and not enough clothing.

"You know I can't ever leave this place. Mason's already in there. It's good to see you." She opens the door to let me in.

I walk down the long hall, lined with people talking and drinking as the music gets louder and louder. So much so, I keep questioning what I'm doing in a place like this. I'm not even sure why I chose it. She only said go out with the guy; it could've been anything. I know I for sure needed a drink, however.

I make my way to the bar for a drink before even attempting to locate Mason amongst the crowd. I stand there patiently until one of the bartenders sees I'm empty-handed. I feel a hand on my shoulder, and I instantly want to go home. I'm just not in the mood to be hit on. But when I turn around, I see it's Reyna. I'm immediately relieved but confused. Did I mess up their plans or something?

"What are you doing here?" I shout in her ear.

"It's the only time I can get my girlfriend out," she shouts back and hands me a drink. "Mason is over there." She points to a group of guys who are sectioned off toward the back of the lounge. I smile, taking my Tom Collins from her hand, and head to the back. It's a little less noisy here, considering the speakers are toward the front.

"The man of the hour!" Mason stands, ready to dap me as I enter the VIP section. "I invited a few friends. Mike, Trev, and Meachum." I shake each of their hands as they are introduced.

"What kind of name is Meachum?" I ask as they all laugh.

"I don't know why this fool got e'ry body calling me by my last name," Meachum responds.

"'Cause it's cool," Mason defends himself.

"And you're a fucking cornball, my dude!" Mike says to Mason.

"Fuck you, man!" Mason laughs.

I chuckle at them, wishing I had close friendships like this. "How do y'all know each other?"

"We went to the university together," Trev answers.

"But this fool up and forgot about his boys now that he's seeing Rey-na," Meachum sings.

Mike and Trev punch Meachum on his arms as Mason bows his head in his hands. I'm not sure why he and Reyna feel they need to keep this a secret, but I already had my suspicions.

"Oh, shit! Was that a secret?" Meachum realizes.

"Ummm, no." I laugh, shoving Mason. "You're good."

For about an hour, I'm able to laugh and actually have a little fun. Phoenix and her lies never even enter my mind. I momentarily believe I'll be able to move on from her. Although, every part of my being dreads the most horrific day of my life.

In a way, I want to get this over with because I don't think I'll be able to take another one of Roselyn's revelations. I feel like the next one will bring hate back into my heart, and Phoenix was the one that brought me out of that darkness. Even though, apparently, she was dealing with her own.

"Yo! There she is!" I hear Trev shout, pointing across the room toward Reyna. But as the crowd around her on the dance floor starts to move away, I see the *her* they're pointing at. However, I can only see her from behind. If I were the same man from before, those hips would have pulled me directly behind her like some pervert.

But I'm not that guy.

This must be the woman Reyna was referring to earlier.

"Damn, that sure is her," Mike adds.

They obviously have been drooling after this woman for some time. But it's not until she sways her hips and turns to face me that I realize I know her. *My her.* The *her* that got away the year before Phoenix. The very first *her* that made me think there could be more than sex to a relationship. Senara Renae.

"That woman is baaad as hell! Damn!" I hear one of the guys say in the background, but I'm too fixated on her swaying to the Reggaeton that's playing. Jeez, that woman has still got it. I'm not sure how, but it seems she's gotten even curvier than the last time I saw her.

Her smile still lights up the room as she entices every onlooker in this place, including me. I adjust my hardened dick as the song goes off, and they disappear in the crowd. She's going to lose her shit if she sees me here. We didn't leave things on the best of terms, even though it was almost three years ago. But as I turn to say goodbye to the fellas, Reyna comes running into our section with Senara in tow.

"Senara, you remember the guys. Trev, Mike, Meachum, and, of course, Mason," Reyna says as she blushes, and Senara waves at them. "And this is..." She swings Senara in front of me.

*Oh boy.*

"Braxton," Senara says. Her stare is blank at first, but it quickly turns to disgust.

"You two know each other?" Reyna asks.

"Unfortunately. I have to go." Senara turns and runs out of the section toward the door.

*Fuck!*

I jump up, charging after her. Not letting her make it too far this time. But those little feet are out the club and halfway down the street much faster than I expected. Luckily, the crowd outside has disbursed now that it's close to closing.

"Senara, wait!" I shout, trying to catch up with her.

"No, Braxton!" She keeps walking, but I'm able to meet her before she makes it into her car.

"Wait!" I place my hand on her car door, keeping her from opening it.

"It's been three years. Are you really still that angry?"

She slowly stares up at me, and those beautiful big brown eyes that I adored before have completely darkened.

"There isn't enough time in this world that'll fix how embarrassed you made me feel."

Every word she said was so impactful it was like she

punched me in the chest. Her stare only intensifies the anger exuding from her, but I refuse to let her go like this. Again.

"Senara, I know I don't deserve to take up any more of your time, but I just want to talk. I'll grovel if I have to."

Her frown begins to dissipate as the light in her eyes finally returns. "I think I'd like to see a little groveling." She giggles.

I'm not sure what comes over me, maybe the fact that I haven't had sex in months, but my urge to feel another woman returned with the sight of her dancing this evening. I lean forward, over her tiny stature, pressing my body against hers. Her telling eyes have always betrayed her, and I know she still wants me. I hope she's single because I don't have time for games.

"I'll gladly get on my knees. My place or yours?" I lean further, hoping she will complete our connection.

Her lustful stare becomes fearful, almost ghostly, and I instantly feel like shit. That or she isn't single and maybe doesn't want me at her house. I back off slightly, giving her enough space to breathe, but not enough to try and run. "Sen, let's just talk. I promise I'll keep my hands to myself." I smile, placing my hands inside of my pockets.

She thinks momentarily, for what seems like an eternity, but I don't want to put any further pressure on her. "I'm pretty hungry. There's a diner right up the street." She looks toward the corner where the light from the diner's sign shines bright enough to light the block.

I see a ton of people, probably from the club, also

heading that way. I'm hoping for some one-on-one time with her. I hadn't realized how much I wanted to see her until she was standing in front of me. Mainly because of how things ended, but more so, because she predicted I would be heartbroken. Just not in this way.

"How about I cook for you? The restaurant is only ten minutes driving time, and you've never been there." I eye her quietly as she discerns whether this is some ploy to get some. So I decide to sweeten the deal. "I can make that grilled cheese you loved so much."

The decision was made quickly as her smile lit up her eyes. She could never turn down my cooking.

"Let's go! Where'd you park?"

"Oh, no. I'll get in the car with you. Don't need you trying to escape." She and I laugh as we get in her Audi and drive to Braxton's on East.

I know I don't have much time before my prep cooks get in here, and I still have to get some sleep. So I waste no time dragging her into the kitchen with me as I make her favorite, grilled cheese with Gouda and bacon. A ten-minute meal that has placed the brightest of smiles on her face. It never really mattered what I put in the sandwich, she's always enjoyed every one. I used to love how happy it made her. I just could never bring myself to show it.

As we ate and sipped a little wine, everything came fluttering back to me. How she squinted her nose whenever I said something really funny, how she slapped my thigh when I was silly, or when she slowly blinked when she started to get sleepy. The one hundred and one little things

I would notice about her in particular back then, but never found the courage to admit. As she slowly begins to blink, I know it's time for the night to end. A night that would end without me even mentioning Phoenix.

"C'mon, let's get you home," I say as I stand, grabbing her hand to lead her out of the restaurant. But she suddenly stops and turns swiftly, bumping right into my chest.

"Forgot something?"

"Yes." She wraps her arms at my neck and jumps up, knowing I would instinctively catch her as I've done many times before. "I did." Before I could stop her, she smothers her tiny lips within my fuller, accepting lips. I don't even think about it, just return her same fervor, excitedly shoving my tongue down her throat.

Our kiss intensifies as she grabs at the back of my neck, grinding her warmth against my now engorged dick. I walk slowly to the bar, placing her down as her dress rises up on its own. I let my lips fall down her cheek and to her neck as she drops her head back, letting me ravenously devour her.

Our bodies now craving for seconds.

Seconds of aggressive foreplay, leading to minutes of lewd pleasure that could possibly give us a second chance of getting this right. Getting us right. I squeeze at her thick thighs, letting my hands slowly glide up her inner thighs as she readily opens them for me.

It's only then that flashes of Phoenix flutter through my brain, invading my need to be with another woman.

The anger from earlier rises along with these thoughts, making me want to continue with Sen in spite of her. I let my thumb slither inside Senara's now soaked, silk panties to find her hardened clit.

"Ah ... I missed those hands, baby," Sen whispers.

But unbeknownst to her, my anger for someone else is imploring me to make Sen cum right now. *Am I using her?* Regardless, my mouth involuntarily slides down further toward her large breasts as my free hand pulls her top down and removes her breasts from her bra in one swift motion.

Before I know it, my lips suckle her hard nipples harshly while I continue to rub her clit harder. She grinds her middle against me as I continue to get what I want from her.

More flashes of Phoenix come to mind in quicker succession, distracting my selfishness. I suddenly remember I'm not this guy anymore. I'm not that same arrogant person who used women because I was angry. I can't do this to her.

Although I know she's about to release, I abruptly pull my finger from her and back away.

"What are you doing?" she asks, panting as if she's just run a mile.

I could barely look up at her, knowing she's about to explode. "I can't do this."

"What? What are you talking about?"

"Senara ... I-I just can't," I respond, knowing she has no

clue about Phoenix and will think I'm embarrassing her again.

"I can't believe this shit!" She quickly fixes her clothes and plops down off the bar to fix her dress. "I can't believe I let you do this to me again!" She walks past me, and I grab for her to try and explain, unable to look her in the eye. "No! Don't you fucking touch me!"

"Sen, it's not what you think," I whisper.

"You're still a fucking coward," she spits, and I finally look up at her bulging brown eyes. Although her words stung. She's right.

"You'll never get this chance again." She stares a moment then stomps out of the restaurant. Leaving me standing there like an idiot once again.

*Fuck!*

# CHAPTER NINE
## Stop Talking

THE NEXT MORNING, I BARELY WANT TO GET OUT OF bed. I'm not sure how I went from pure anger at one point of the day to letting another woman, possibly my second chance in more ways than one, get close to me. *Close to me for what fucking reason?* So I can be tortured by my dead ex's memory yet again? What the fuck is wrong with me? It's only been a year. God forbid I finally try and move on.

I roll out of bed, thinking of the last words Senara spoke to me, just as damning as before. I'll never have the chance to be with her or anyone else for that matter. Why should I even fucking bother? I'm damned if I do, damned if I don't.

I finally sit up, pushing myself to shower so I can get myself to work. I'm glad I decided to get my car last night instead of rushing to get it this morning. Now that I've gotten my desire to cook back and my passion for making people smile because of my food, I need to focus on the business, possibly reopening the other restaurant. Whatever happens, happens.

Right now, I need to be prepared for Bynum's unexpected visit. I still haven't decided what to make.

By the time I make it to the restaurant, it's almost time for the lunch crowd. Luckily, I've hired a dependable staff and don't need to do basically anything to prepare. "OH, my God. Where have you been?!" Reyna appears in front of me from nowhere as I walk in the door. Her eyes frantic as she pulls me to the side, out of view. "I've been calling you for the last fifteen minutes."

I pull out my phone only to realize I never charged it, and it's completely dead. Still unclear about whatever the big emergency is, I shrug my shoulders and put my phone back in my pocket. God, I hope this isn't about her friend that apparently didn't realize I was the chef she worked for. How, I don't know. "Well, what's the problem?"

"That's the problem." She steps back and points behind her. I look into the restaurant to see Julia Bynum fixing her hair in a tiny mirror.

"Shit! She never does this during lunch. Why's she here?"

"Apparently, Little Miss Hot Shot is too busy for the tiny people now. She can only fit us in for lunch."

This totally ruins the meal I had attempted to plan for her. It'll have to be simple but mind-blowing. I think hard, trying to think of what my patrons always loved on the menu, and it hits me. *Grilled Cheese.* I picture Senara's smile last night, which saddens me for a moment, but I decide to use this to my advantage.

"Mason has already begun braising short ribs for dinner tonight, right?"

She smiles, nodding her head excitedly. She loves my ribs, and I've only told Mason my secret to making them the tastiest and juiciest. Just thinking about those juices mixed with the cheese is making me hungry. Or it could be because I skipped breakfast this morning.

"We got this!" I wink at her before making my way over to Bynum, who hurriedly puts the mirror away and stands to shake my hand. She certainly seems to have come a long way from her appearance alone. She's much more put together, even a little fancy for a Tuesday afternoon. No ball cap and jeans today.

"Mr. Knight, I see you're still as handsome as ever." She blushes as we shake hands.

"You're looking pretty good yourself, Julia." She turns even redder as she takes her seat.

"You arrive pretty late for a chef," she pokes.

"Umm, long morning, but I thought maybe I'd actually sit and have lunch with you since I made you wait so long."

Her smile widens. "Do I smell a personal interview and lunch? I've never had the opportunity."

"I know. So what do you think?"

She doesn't even hesitate, "I can't wait."

"I'll be right back." I smile, grabbing Reyna as I walk away.

"Get her one of Reggie's Sea Breezes and keep her occupied."

She nods and scurries toward the bartender, who has only been with us about a year. We lucked out on finding him on short notice after our last one just up and disappeared.

In the back, I barely speak to anyone, as I'm sure they all know Bynum's in, and I'll be in the zone. I ask Mason to fry up some of our homemade potato chips for two as I pull together the ingredients for the best braised short rib grilled cheese on sourdough she's ever had in her life. I try not to get too distracted as I cook, but the thoughts of what kinds of questions she might ask worry me.

How much does she know about my personal and business life? I tried to keep the two separated, of course, but this past year caused me to screw up both. Although my business is on the mend, my personal life is just as jacked up and lonely, maybe even more so now, as it was with her first visit. However, the first time she came, I also met Phoenix.

So it became a blessing for my business and pleasure. Who knows? Maybe it could happen again.

Finally finished with her meal, Mason helps me plate the two dishes before I hurriedly bring them out to her. Going through the doors, I see she has already set up her portable lighting and camera, and then I realize she intends to go live for this one as well. I'm not sure I want people to see me stuffing my face and trying to talk.

Carefully, I pay close attention to what's in front of me

only. I don't need a complete repeat of last time. That may not go over as well. I place our plates down just as she finishes her drink, so I ask Reyna to bring her another and an Uptown for me.

"Oh, crap, that looks good!" She smiles, pulling a napkin apart, and places it on her lap. "You ready?" she asks as she sticks her phone inside the stand of the circular light.

"As ready as I can be." I plop the napkin on my lap.

She hits the live button on her phone and situates herself as people quickly join. "Hey, beauties! It's that time again, as promised. I'm back at Braxton's on East as you lovely people requested, to catch up with the one and only Braxton Knight." She points at me, and I wave like a buffoon, not knowing what else to do. She then lifts her plate up to show her meal. "Look, my lunch has arrived safely, and to my table too!" We both laugh, easing the tension as I see her live numbers already reach five thousand in less than two minutes.

"Yes, we don't need a repeat of last time."

"Well, not the mess, but the great-tasting food ... absolutely." She smiles, nodding at me. "Not only that, peeps, but our Knight has decided to eat lunch with us and have a bit of a conversation. So let's get started." She picks up one half of the sandwich, and I watch her take a slow bite. I anxiously wait for a reaction, which seems to take forever. I watch Reyna from the corner of my eyes await the same reaction.

"I swear," Bynum continues to chew, "this man can never disappoint me." She giggles then takes another bite.

I breathe as Reyna jumps up and down quietly, happy Bynum's sudden intervention was a success. The food is so good, in fact, I think she forgot she had an audience watching her, and forgot to chew.

"Ugh, this is so good. I barely want to stop and speak." She laughs. "But I'm sure the ladies want to know what's been up with you. So let's chat."

She asks as many questions as she likes while we enjoy our meal. I try hard not to give too many bullshit answers and just be myself. All I need is something else to happen that will embarrass the shit out of me.

As the interview winds down, she settles herself in her chair and wipes her mouth with the napkin on her lap, then tosses it on her empty plate.

"So, how have you been holding up?" she asks.

My eyes widen at the concern on her face, and I know she's talking about Phoenix. With the question, I see Reyna attempt to walk over to end the interview. I'm not sure how she even heard Bynum from over there, but I'm sure she thought I would lose my shit in High Definition. I hold my hand up so she can see, beneath the table.

"It's been difficult. I'm not going to lie. You make all these plans for the future with someone, and then everything is snatched away with no warning." I drop my head and fight back the tears. No one needs to see this on a man.

She places her hand on my thigh, and then quickly

removes it. "I can't even imagine the feelings. It's been about a year now since Phoenix's death. I'm sure there have been women rivaling to take her place."

I instantly think of Senara. She's really been the only woman I've been willing to give the time of day to this entire grieving period. I'm not going to lie, there have been plenty of women that have thrown themselves at me, but there's no way I can go from Phoenix to a fling.

"There's one woman in particular, but I'm pretty sure I messed that up," I admit to the camera.

"Please. You're Braxton Knight. I'm sure whatever you've done, it's nothing flowers and an apology can't fix," she laughs. "Well, that's it, folks. Come back to Braxton's on East, and I guarantee you won't be disappointed." She waves at the phone, and I do the same before she presses the button to end the broadcast. She quickly disassembles her light and stand. "Thank you so much, Braxton. That was pretty much perfect. And," she points to the empty plate in front of her, "you need to put that on the menu."

"I just may have to." I stand as she picks up her things. "Thanks for the exposure again, Julia," I say, shaking her hand.

Well, that didn't go nearly as bad as the last time or expected.

"Braxton!" Reyna comes over to me with her reservations book. "We're already booked for the next month!" I smile, finally believing something good actually came from listening to Roselyn.

"I guess I should get in the kitchen then."

SECONDS

The day ends up being a complete blur. I'm completely unprepared for the crowd that followed Bynum's broadcast, all asking for that grilled cheese even at dinner.

I went viral all over again. And I loved every second of it. Hearing the frustrations and commotion echoing through the kitchen brought my spirit back to life. Me back to life. Apparently, my phone too.

Once Reyna charged it, she was on it all day, replying to as many texts, calls, and direct messages as she could. I almost felt bad for her, but the big smile on her face tells me she is satisfied in her element, and I am too. After all, her handling my social media and business is all part of her job.

By the end of the night, I am completely exhausted and just want a hot shower and a bed. I'm so tired, I don't even think about Phoenix or plan to while I'm home. All I can think about is my king-sized bed.

I wrap things up as my staff leaves for the night.

"Today was a great day." Reyna hands me my phone. "I've set up a few more interviews for you over the next couple of weeks for cooking networks. Who knows, maybe you'll even get one of your own cooking shows."

I laugh out. "God, I hope not!"

"Most people were interested in this mystery woman you were talking about ... anything to do with last night?" She smirks sneakily, hoping I'd be willing to divulge whatever is going on with Senara and me. Clearly, Senara has not.

"Oh, no, you don't. I'll see you tomorrow, Ms. Reyna. I'm sure you and Mason have plans." I smile as she blushes and runs out of here before I press for details.

As I remove my chef jacket and grab my keys, I hear the kitchen door swing open again.

"Forget something?" I ask with my back turned.

"Hi," I hear a faint whisper, and I know immediately it's not Reyna.

I turn to see her standing at the entrance, big brown eyes, waiting for permission to come in further. But my eyes roaming her body causes me to lose my manners briefly. I admire her intently in her tight, low-cut jeans and cutoff tank, her long hair in a ponytail.

"Hi," I respond simply, not knowing what else to say. I don't move, however, in fear I won't be able to control my loins, and we'll have a repeat of last night.

"I'm not going to take up too much of your time." She pauses to wait for me to say something, but I'm not sure what to say.

"I'm in no rush." I place the keys on the counter and stand in place with my hands in my pockets.

"I just want to tell you I had no idea about your girlfriend. Had I known, I would've understood what happened last night. Now, I just feel like I behaved like a brat, and you didn't deserve that. I mean, obviously, you've changed now," she continues to ramble on.

I hear the words, but I somewhat stopped listening the

moment her beautiful, tiny lips started to move. The fact that she showed up here unexpectedly only proves to me that I need to see what happens. It's like the idea of Sen and me being together keeps presenting itself, and I keep fucking it up. But I feel like it's now or never.

As she continues to mumble about everyone having secrets, I walk up to her and grab her face in my hands, so that she's forced to shut the fuck up and look at me. "Sen, stop talking."

I lean forward and kiss her softly, not wanting to become too excited and end up fucking her on this countertop ... visions or no. I pull away from her and stare down at her softened brown eyes. "I think we should give this a try."

She smiles. "Okay." Lifting her hands behind my neck, she pulls me in for a deeper kiss. One full of passion and a longing to explore what our relationship could possibly become.

# CHAPTER TEN

## Expletives

THE NEXT DAY WAS MY APPOINTMENT WITH WEST. I HAD so much to divulge in such a short period of time, but I've been thinking about moving on all night. This is something I have to do, but I don't want to mess things up. The best way for me not to do that is to deal with what happened to Phoenix. This would require me to actually not let my animosity get the best of me. Something that has been difficult, to say the least.

I mean, our relationship, if I can call it that, may have been secretive and short-lived, but I've never fallen for someone so hard in my life. I knew I was in trouble when I told her about my parents. I have never told anyone about my mother's betrayal to anyone. The reason I've had a hard time letting anyone in, but if I've learned nothing else from being with Phoenix, I've accepted that love sometimes can be painful. If I close my heart off to it completely, I'm only hurting myself.

Once I get to Roselyn West's office, I knock on the door instead of barging in. Today will be the last day I learn something about Phoenix before our next visit. The visit where I'll be forced to talk about it. I'm determined not to leave here pissed.

After all, how much could I have really known about the woman I chose to give my all to, who couldn't do the same in return? I constantly think about our last month together. The only time in the entire year of our relationship where I was able to take her off the grounds of her home. The time after she told her father about us. The person who I assumed was actually keeping us apart. I even got her back into my restaurant the night before her death. Now I just feel like we should have kept our desires a damn secret.

"Come in, Braxton," West says, assuming it is me knocking.

I enter her office as she stands to round her desk and sits in her seat across the couch.

"I thought I'd be more civilized today, instead of colliding into the door like some raging bull." I chuckle.

"Well, at least we know you *can* be civil." She laughs as I lie back on the couch. "So, tell me. How did it go?"

"So," I turn my head to face her, "you were right, as usual. I did need to get out of the house. It was relaxing being out with Mason and his friends. It reminded me that I can still have fun." I turn my head back and stare at the ceiling.

"Great! For a second when you left, I knew you would find a reason to just go home and-,"

"I ran into Senara," I blurt out as she rambles in mid-sentence. I knew she would know exactly who that was because Phoenix brought her up for some reason when we started coming here that last month we were together.

She clears her throat and adjusts in her seat, ready to write whatever I say next. "And how did that go?"

"As expected at first, but things turned when I tried to take things further ... sexually."

"Uh-huh. How so?" Her voice is monotone.

I sit up abruptly. "Yo, I really wanted to. When I saw her, everything came flooding back. I know Phoenix would tell me Senara was the one that got away, but I didn't actually realize it until we started talking again. Everything that attracted me to her ... those eyes, her smile—oh, my God, her laugh." I stand and walk over to her glass doors to peer out into her yard. A view I always look at for some reason.

"Braxton, what happened when you tried to become intimate?"

"Phoenix happened. I became infuriated, as if being with Senara would somehow punish a dead woman." I turn to face West. "I'm clearly delusional."

"You're definitely not. Only human. You feel betrayed. You also knew Senara is the only other woman who could hold a torch next to Phoenix. And so did Phoenix."

I sit back down, looking at the floor. "I know you're right, but when I stopped things from going further, Senara was pissed. I truly thought that was it."

"And how did you feel about that?"

"Like a piece of shit, obviously. Luckily, when Bynum came to the restaurant, she learned things she didn't know." I perk up suddenly. "Did you see the interview?"

She smiles widely. "I did. My husband is much more into social media than I am and showed me. Can I assume Senara is the woman you were referring to at the end?"

I nod. "It brought her back to me. I don't want to mess this up. We agreed to take things slow last night, but my hands are becoming more and more grabby these days around her." We both laugh. "I just want to get a handle on things so I can move on."

"Sounds like a plan. We'll get through today, and in a couple of weeks, we can get down to business."

I eye her curiously. "A couple of weeks?"

"Vacation, remember?"

"Ugh! You really don't need a vacation." I chuckle.

"Mr. Knight, I need a vacation from just you alone." She laughs, standing to grab her tea from her desk. "Now that you're ready to move on, in a way, let's talk about the last month. What ultimately brought the two of you here?"

I'm not always pleased about how that happened because she saw a side of me I never intended to show. Not toward her anyway. Everything didn't just come to a head at that time; it was a buildup of things. It really happened the first time I was able to actually go inside her house.

*It had been six months of our weekly picnics when Phoenix said she had a surprise for me. I'm sure she sensed my annoyance building due to our secret relationship and not being able to take her out. Be seen in public. Not only that, but we can't just hang out in her yard forever. We're two very grown people, and I was done with the high school games.*

*But that day after her "Good Morning" text, she told me to just drive straight up to the front door, as opposed to parking just outside of her dead-end street. I assumed she finally came clean, and I was about to be hounded by her parents.*

*I timidly walk up to her front door just as the door flies open. Before I know what's happened, this tiny person with a ton of hair comes flying at my face. She throws her arms around my neck and kisses me hard as she grabs at the back of my head. I reciprocate, returning her same fervor.*

*"What about your guard? Your parents?" I ask, pulling away from her.*

*She pulls me inside her home, and I barely pay attention to the massive foyer littered with artifacts that seem to be symbolic for her culture. She leads me directly to the indoor elevator and pushes a button before shoving me against the back of the elevator car.*

*I've never seen this aggressive side of her, and even though this wouldn't be the first time we've had sex, it would be the first time in her home. But I can't help but feel like she's still sneaking me around. I'm so done with it.*

*"What about the cameras?" I push her back gently.*

*"Why are you asking so many questions?" she snaps.*

*Between her aggression and her flushed skin, I'm too turned on to think so much. Over the last few months, she's learned to express* herself thoroughly in more ways than one. I'm not sure when I became such a fucking chick, but that's not what she obviously needs right now. Clearly, she wants my dick plunged deep inside of her, not some whiny bitch.

Just then, the elevator dings, and I peer behind her, directly into her room and right at her large bed. I pick her up to my waist without a word and smother her lips with mine. She grinds against me hard as I approach her bed and toss her onto it. She quickly grabs at the hair tie on her wrist to put her extremely long hair into a bun. Something she always does, and I hate I'm unable to pull at it.

"No! Leave it!" I pull my shirt over my head and toss it to the floor. "Turn around and bend over."

She excitedly does what she's told, arching her back just as she's learned I like.

I lean forward over her, so I'm close to her ear. "Let's see how wet you are for me." I take two of my fingers and slide them through the slick slit of her warmth from front to back as she jolts at the sensation of my touch. "Hmm, almost," I whisper.

I stand quickly and drop to my knees before grabbing at her legs, pulling her closer to the edge and pushing her sheer nightgown up. Without hesitation, I smash my face between the back of her thighs and shove my tongue directly on her clit.

"Agh!" She jumps, trying to get away from me, but I hold her legs in place as I taste her juices.

She's never been able to take me eating her pussy, so this is extra gratifying now that I'm so ferociously ravenous at the moment. And there's nowhere for her to go this time. She begins to gyrate against me as she pleads for me to stop, but this is what she wants.

*I'm tired of feeling like I'm being controlled. Kept on a leash. Handled. She's going to be fucking handled. I'm done feeling like she's got the upper hand, and I'm just a fucking game.*

"Braxton! Oh-"

She doesn't finish her expletive for whatever reason, but it doesn't matter because I taste her warm juices as they fill my throat. I stand, retrieving a condom from my pocket, and drop my pants before adjusting her back into position, not giving her the slightest chance to catch her breath. Hurriedly, I remove the condom from its wrapper, slide it on quickly, and jab my dick inside of her as she squeals. I wrap her long, thick hair around my fist and part of my wrist. I pull her head back slightly and grab her ass cheek with the other and begin to thrust deeper into what has become mine.

She begins to back her ass up against my pelvis as the echoing of our skin colliding bounces from the walls. I pull her head back further, squeezing her ass tighter as I grind into her wetness harder. Her aggressive growling from the intense pleasure only excites me more, but my anger is still very present.

It has elevated to the point that I can barely concentrate. Even now, she's pulling my strings to get exactly what she wants. *I'm a man, so in this instance, I'm willing to give in. But I'm not doing this anymore. I'm nobody's fucking doormat.*

I pound into her forcefully as she screams out my name. I feel her body begin to tremble, and I'm ready for her to cum as I do the same. Without hesitation, I release her long locks and push her off of me softly. I pull the condom off and look around her room to see if there's something I can use to wrap it in.

"You can throw it in the toilet," she whispers as she turns on her back and finally pulls her hair into a bun.

I do as she says, entering her large pink and black bathroom and flushing the condom in the toilet. As I walk out, I stop at the sink to toss water on my face. The bathroom reminds me of the hotel I used to stay in before I moved here to Maryland.

I grab one of the pink and black rags from the rack and dry my face. Staring in the vanity-like mirror, I think about the last blowup I had with a woman. A woman who just wanted to be near me and I pushed her away. Something she didn't deserve.

Now, here I am feeling the exact same way. Betrayed. Used ... I'm not that guy. That pouty guy that demands to be appreciated. I feel the rage rise the longer I stare into the mirror and an explosion coming on. I take a deep breath and step back into her bedroom. She has taken the thin nightgown she was wearing off and is in a matching bra and panty set.

Why does she have to make it so difficult?

She stares at me timidly as I lean in the doorway, taking in the lavishness of her room. She has photos of herself and friends all over the walls. I assume these are from college before she told me she got expelled due to the consequences of drinking. These are also people she talks about, but I have never met. I doubt they even know about me.

However, I do notice most of these pictures are taken here or when she was on campus. Her life seems to be spent captive under what her parents allow her to do. And that's it. I'm not sure this is something I can accept. I need her to get out of this house, but she has to want to. I decide to broach the conversation with her at a distance.

"We need to talk," I say.

She sits up on the bed, folding her legs in. "Okay. Do you want to know how I got you in here or something?"

That's not the issue because I shouldn't have to sneak in here, but I'm curious. "Yeah, we can start there."

"I called a friend to get him to loop the footage, and I knew Bear had to go with my parents for the day."

I shake my head. "This is the problem. I'm tired of this. You're a grown woman. I'm a grown-ass man. I'm not doing this anymore."

"You're not doing what?" she slides to the end of the bed, staring nervously.

"You know what. This!" I span the room and the space between us. "You need to stand up to your parents and stop being trapped in a cage."

"Braxton, it's more to it than that."

"Okay," I step forward, "Explain it. What am I missing?"

She doesn't respond at first, but glares down at her white carpet, letting her feet dangle from the high bed. "I can't tell you that," she finally whispers.

"You can't tell me?" I repeat the question, annoyed, and begin to walk toward her, but stop just in front of her. "Maybe you're not hearing me. I'm not doing this anymore. Leave with me right now, or I'm leaving alone for good."

I impatiently wait for her to respond. I hear her begin to sniffle when a tear falls down her cheek. I swiftly feel the need to take it all back, but I can't. We need to deal with this now.

"Please." She stands, trying to reach for me, but I back away. "There are things about my family no one can know. About how we got all this." She waves around the room. "How I'm needed to make sure we maintain this."

I have no idea what she's talking about, but clearly, she has some sort of responsibility to her family. I honestly can care less though. I need some sort of give. "Okay. Fine. So tell me what that is. I need to know something. Any fucking thing."

She takes a deep breath as she begins to sob. "I can't tell you that."

"Well, you've made your choice." I grab my shirt from the floor and slide it over my head as I turn to walk away from her. Away from us and whatever lies she wants to tell.

"Braxton, don't! I love you!" she shouts.

I stop in my stride at the sound of those three words. The three words she's shown, but never spoken. The reason I can't continue to do this. "I love you too, Phoenix," I whisper without turning to face her. "That's just not enough anymore."

I sigh deeply and leave her room, head down the stairs beside the elevator, and directly out of her dreadful family home.

I never got the chance to go back there willingly, but it turned out that moment wasn't the end of us. The four months it took her to do what I needed was torturous. I didn't see anyone else. Instead, buried my head into my restaurant and the launch of the third. I became so busy time eventually got away from me until she stood in front of me at my restaurant just as I was closing. She looked horrible as if the light in her eyes dissipated with each day that we were apart. She wasn't the same woman I remember, more damaged and scared. That's when I knew without one word from her that she did what I asked.

She steps forward after I hadn't said anything for what seemed to be minutes.

"Hi," she whispers.

Without a thought, I grab and pull her into my chest, and she squeezes me tight as her tears start to soak my shirt.

"Took you long enough." I kiss her on the top of the head.

"I hope I'm not too late." She looks up at me by placing her chin on my chest.

I wipe the tears from her face, then run my fingers down her long ponytail. "It was like time stood still for you." I smile.

Her cheeks turn crimson as she stands on her toes to kiss me. And I reciprocate, kissing her softly as if time is now on our side.

"I have to ask, are we officially out in the open? Can I flaunt you as mine like I've wanted to do since day one?"

She giggles. "Flaunt away, my Knight. I'm all yours."

## CHAPTER ELEVEN

### Use My Words

"Obviously, that's what brought us here. She told me she started seeing you, and you helped her find the words to finally tell her parents that she had to live her own life. She told me that for whatever reason, her father believed Phoenix has cursed them and disowned her after that," I say, not wanting to go any further into that month with her.

West put her notepad down and leaned forward in her seat, taking a deep breath. "She brought you here because I told her to. You were obviously important, but I also felt you needed to know the full truth about them. Her parents. Her family."

"I know that. I'd like to finally know everything."

"Yes, but because you don't want to talk about why she's not here anymore today, I won't tell you everything."

"So, I was right!" I stand. "Her parents are the real reason she's gone!"

"Not exactly. But because of their business and certain choices, she was promised to someone who did not have her best interest at heart."

"Then ... it was her stalker. The guy she was engaged to the entire time we were together." I stop myself, not wanting to let the rage build further. I sit back down. "Just tell me whatever it is you're trying to say."

"Her family is big in the 'charity world.'" She uses air quotes and sighs. "But they had to do some unsavory things to get to where they are now."

"I have no idea what you're talking about," I snap, wondering why she's beating around the bush.

"All I can tell you is her father is ingrained within the political scene here in Maryland. They are known for getting things done."

I just find it difficult to see Phoenix amongst these types of people. When we first began, she was so timid and fragile ... fearful of her family. Now I just feel like my interference caused all of this to happen. I could tell from her father's impromptu visit he was absolutely furious. My disdain for him trying to control his daughter only fueled my need to keep her away from him.

"And her stalker? Where does he fit in all of this?"

"She always told me her father first gained notoriety for his noble attempts to gain rights for the Native Americans. He had great intentions. Eventually, it became more about power and control. Her stalker's family would enhance that power. With both family names, he'd be unstoppable. Until you."

"Yes. Until me," I repeat, fully accepting my role but trying hard not to take full blame. That wouldn't be fair to myself or Phoenix's memory. I realize that now. But I'm still curious. "Do you think if her father knew her fiancé," I roll my eyes as the word rolls off my tongue, "abused Phoenix, he would still force the marriage?"

"Frankly, yes. He loved his daughter, but he *needed* power and control. Phoenix knew this."

I drop my head, understanding how alone she must have felt. I'd like to believe I gave her a voice when I came into her life. I just wish that voice hadn't also ended her life.

"Is there a reason you're not telling me who her stalker is?"

"You're not ready. Our next visit, I will have to tell you. I just need you to do this one thing for me while I'm away."

*Oh boy!*

"I guess this is my homework?"

She giggles. "Yes. For the next two weeks, I want you to let go of this. Give yourself fully to Senara and let her in. Can you do that?"

I'm not sure how to answer that. Over the past few days, I've been able to live my life outside of Phoenix's constant shadow. But an entire two weeks is another story. Not only that, but I also have to tell Sen everything about Phoenix, so she knows what she's getting into. I don't want her to think she's the rebound woman. She's already much more than that.

"Once I tell Sen everything, I promise to make it only about her and me."

"Good. You should do that. Boy, have you come a long-long-long-long—"

"Oh, all right! I get it." We both laugh as I stand to ready myself to leave. "Enjoy your time away from me." I smile.

"I certainly will." She giggles as I wave good-bye.

As I get in the car, I decide it's best to get everything out in the open. As soon as possible.

Me: **Sen, we need to talk.**

I wait patiently for her to respond. Then I realize that's never a good text to send. When I start to clear it up, she responds.

Senara: **Uh oh. That's never good.**

Me: **Can I come over?**

Senara: **No**

She responds much faster.

Senara: **I'd rather come to your place. Can't tonight, but tomorrow after your dinner service?**

Me: **I'll send the address and time. See ya then, boo!**

Now I have to go home and make it presentable. I hope I'll be able to keep my hands off of her long enough to actually use my words.

# CHAPTER TWELVE

## Punch Him in the Face and Bounce

THE DAY SEEMED TO DRAG THE MORE I ANTICIPATED ME and Sen's late-night date. I decide to bring home some of the dessert I made for tonight's menu since I'm sure she's already eaten dinner. I had every intention of showering before she came, but as I step out of my car, I get a message from her saying she's already in the lobby.

My heart palpitates in anticipation of seeing her for the first time since the night of the interview. Although we've been texting nonstop, it seems there's nothing like looking into the eyes that see right through me.

I quickly grab the bag with our dessert and walk up the flight of stairs from the parking lot to the lobby of my building.

"Mr. Knight," the concierge sees me immediately, "you have a visitor, sir."

"Thank you, John." I smile at her as she walks toward

us, looking as beautiful as ever. I look at John. "You may let her into my place whenever she's here."

"Will do, sir," John responds.

"Shall we?" I extend my arm to Sen, who happily grabs it with both of her hands. I walk her into the elevator and press my code to get into my penthouse suite.

I bought this place after I went viral the first time, earning quite a bit of money from all the appearances. Turns out, it was a good investment because this past year, I unfortunately lost a lot too.

We ride up the elevator in silence, and I let her walk into my place once the elevator dings and opens. She only takes two steps inside and just looks around in shock. She never really knew how much money I made before Braxton's on East opened, but she knew I did well for myself. That has grown exponentially within the three years she's been out of my life.

I've only ever let Phoenix up here, though. My home has always been my solace until I couldn't share it with the woman I loved anymore.

"It's okay to go in," I joke.

She turns to face me, then back at my spacious living room with over twelve-foot ceilings and black and white furniture. As she continues to look around, I go into my kitchen to put the cheesecake in the refrigerator; I grab some wine and glasses before finding her.

Once I come out, she's already made it to the fireplace mantle. The mantle that holds photos of Phoenix and me. I usually can't bring myself to look at them, but

I decide to take this opportunity to start the conversation.

"I was trying to teach her how to cook. That was a fail." I chuckle as she holds the picture I took of Phoenix removing her burned baked chicken from the oven. Something I thought would be simple but turned out to be disastrous.

"I'm sorry. I didn't mean to snoop." She quickly puts the picture back on the brick mantle.

"You're good." I take her hand and lead her out onto my wrap-around balcony. She stands at the railing as I open the wine and pour her a glass of Moscato.

"It's so beautiful," she whispers, staring out into the city.

"I'd say so." I hand her the glass as I wink at her.

"Smooth, Knight, but I don't think I need any cheese with this wine," she jokes.

"Oh, you callin' me cheesy?" We both laugh.

"Well, if the shoe fits."

"Hmm." I take a sip of wine and stand behind her. I place my hands at either side of her, press my dick against her plump bottom, and lean down to her ear. "I think we fit pretty well," I whisper in her ear as I slightly grind against her.

She turns swiftly and stares up at me, taking another sip of her wine. Our proximity is so close, I can smell the scent of her intoxicating perfume as it blows around us. I stare down at her, wanting to let her in, but I will not be able to handle lies or being used. So I'm going to start by telling her everything I need to and hope she realizes I don't need another heartbreak.

"What do you need to talk about?" she asks, breaking our silence.

"Phoenix," I admit quickly.

"I thought that might be it." She takes my hand this time and sits on the couch behind us, and I follow.

"Once I saw the interview, I looked up whatever I could find on you two. We don't have to go into detail."

"So, you know how?" I ask.

"I do. I'm so sorry," she consoles, touching my thigh. "I'm sure that was hard, losing someone so abruptly."

"I don't talk about that." I look out toward the skyline. "I just wanted you to know I'm not the same person I was. I'm dealing with things... seeing a therapist. Needless to say, Phoenix had a lot of secrets. Fed me a few lies." I glance away from Sen again. "I don't want to harbor any resentment anymore. Any anger."

"I understand, Braxton. I assumed that's why you wanted to take things slow. That's fine with me."

"Also," I look her straight in the eye, "I plan to, or would like to, really see where this goes. That means total honesty, and we have to let each other in. Really get to know each other for who we are now."

I wait for her to respond as she breaks eye contact with me. I impulsively want to think she's keeping something from me, but instead of thinking the worst, I decide to believe she just doesn't want me to hurt her again.

"Sen..." I use my pointer finger to lift her head back up.

"You can trust me with your heart. Just trust me enough to let me break down the walls you have guarding it."

She nods her head, and I take that as acceptance. I smile at her before taking her wine glass from her and placing them on the table in front of us.

"C'mere," I say, pulling her hand and left leg over to straddle me. I cup her cheeks in my hands as she stares down at me. Her eyes illuminated by the moonlight shining down on us. "Thank you."

She smiles as I pull her down to kiss her softly. Our connection is slow and deliberate, not wanting to rush, but feel the intensity of our attraction to each other. Hoping we can turn this into something much more. Much deeper.

Tonight, Senara makes love to me, signifying her letting the past go, and I do the same. The devotion between us is explored through the connection of our bodies, and I enjoy every uninterrupted moment of it.

---

From that night on and for every night the next two weeks, we either spend the night together in each other's arms or on the phone, listening to each other breathe like we were in high school. I did exactly as the doctor ordered with no regrets or guilt.

However, there is one thing that has continued to irk me. Ever since the first night we ran into each other at Chasers until now, she has kept me from her place. She claimed it was because she moved back in with her parents shortly after we stopped seeing each other because she fell on hard times.

She's lying.

Because we agreed to be honest, I asked her again if there was anything she was keeping from me, and she told me no. So, I let it go.

I thought about talking to West about it, but I know she would tell me to get out of my head. I look at my watch, knowing I could wait a couple of hours to speak with West in person, but I still found myself here, sitting outside of Senara's parents' house.

I don't know how I remembered the address from the one time I picked her up after one of her family's Sunday dinners. Dinners she tried to trap me with before. Either she's in there, or she's not.

Me: *Are you home?*

Senara: *Yeah, sweets. Are we still on tonight?*

I don't respond. Instead, I get out of the car and walk slowly across the street. As I stand in front of the house, my worries tell me to turn around and go. But I just can't. I have to know. If she's telling the truth, I will do everything in my power to smooth things over with her. If there's another man in the house, I'll just punch him in the face once and bounce. *I think that would make me feel better.*

I finally find my footing and walk up to the large blue door that stands between me and my next decision. I knock on the door and patiently wait for someone to answer.

"I'll be right there," I hear Senara's voice through the

door, and I feel somewhat relieved she is at least where she claims to be.

The door suddenly opens wide, and I see Senara's shocked face, which quickly turns to fear.

*Oh no!*

My heart drops, and I immediately know I'm about to lose it. As she begins to open her mouth to speak, I hear small patting of tiny feet running to the door. I look down to see a young boy, squeezing his tiny body between the door and Senara, then stands in front of her, looking up at me.

*What the fuck?*

I can't punch this little guy in the face. I bend down so that I'm able to look him in the eye, and I swear it's like glancing in a mirror.

"Hey, Lil' Man," I say with a smile.

He grabs at Senara, wedging as close to her as possible, but still smiles at me.

Senara bends down. "Braxton, go back inside with Grammy and Pop-Pop."

The little one with my name waves at me before running back inside. Senara and I both stand up simultaneously as I step back onto the porch, and she closes the door.

She doesn't say anything as I try to process what just happened. I can hear her take tiny steps toward me and stop as I lean my hands on the railing of the front porch. Rage rises within me as I put it together. But I keep landing on the conversation we just had two weeks prior. I turn around and face her, her eyes filled with tears and regret. She fumbles with her fingers but doesn't look away from me.

"So, I guess it was you I couldn't trust with my heart," I say simply and walk away from her.

"Braxton, wait!" she shouts from her porch, but I'm already at my car, driving away from another woman I thought would never hurt me ... and apparently, my son.

# CHAPTER THIRTEEN

## Dead Eyes

I FIND MYSELF STEWING, SITTING AT THE EDGE OF MY bed. A ton of questions begin to burrow at me. Questions I deserve answers to, but I'm too damn angry to get them. I start doing the mental math, thinking I could have been wrong, but then quickly remember she named him Braxton.

*I can't believe she did this shit!*

What if we never saw each other at the bar? Would I still not know? How could she continue to keep this from me and lie daily straight to my face?! Especially after I basically bared my goddamn soul to her. That fucking bitch!

Just then, I hear the ding of my elevator and know it can only be her. She's got some fucking nerve. I remain seated as I hear her walk around my home looking for me. I could just go in my panic room since I hadn't mentioned that to her yet; that would make me the coward she thought I was three years ago. Obviously, she thought I was a fucking deadbeat too!

She makes her way into the bedroom but stops at the door when she sees me sulking.

"Can we talk?" she asks.

I stand to walk toward her. "The time for talking was three years ago when you found out you were pregnant." I look down directly into her eyes and walk past her. I hear her follow close behind.

"I understand that you're upset—"

"Oh, I'm fucking pissed!" I roar, turning abruptly to face her. "You kept my son from me ... you've been lying to my face." I close my eyes as they begin to water like a fucking punk. "You made me fall for you after knowing what I went through."

She begins to sob. "Braxton, I-I'm sorry. I was going to call you, but I couldn't bring myself to tell you. Then it became harder and harder the longer I waited."

"That's some selfish-ass bullshit, Senara, and you know it. Tell me, if I hadn't come back around, would he have grown up thinking his father was a piece of shit?!"

She looks at the floor, not sure how to answer my question. The tears fall heavier down her face, but I'm not in a place to console her. I have no clue what to do with this shit. What I do know is I need to get the fuck away from her.

"As far as I'm concerned, you're a fucking liar." I saunter over to the kitchen counter to grab my car key. "I expect you gone when I get back." I don't wait for her to say a word. I want to put as much distance between us as possible.

I check my watch, grateful it's time for my appointment with West. Once I arrive at her office, I walk to the door, prepared to bolt in as usual, but the door is already open. I saunter in to see her sitting at her desk, dressed down, no makeup, and completely tan. She looks replenished, and I feel jealous right away. I wanted to feel as I felt yesterday walking in here today. But that's just not the case. I sit on the couch without a word, not knowing where to start.

"Braxton? Are you okay?" She stands and walks toward me, but I don't answer her. "Are you that concerned about today's conversation?"

*I wish!*

"I have a son," I whisper to the floor.

She sits beside me, something else she never does. "What do you mean, you have a son?"

I look over at her. "Senara got pregnant three years ago and never told me. I found out today."

"You found out? So she didn't tell you?"

I huff. "No." I stand, facing the door to her backyard with my hands in my pockets. "When am I going to learn that women can't be trusted?"

"Don't go back there, Braxton."

I turn to face her. "Why do I try? I did exactly as you said. I told her everything. I let her in, and for what?"

"Braxton, I'm going to need you to have a seat and take a breath." She stands and points at the couch.

As I sit, she goes over to her desk and grabs an envelope before sitting in her chair across from me.

"I'm not sure I can talk about this today," I whisper.

"Too bad. Now is the time."

I lean back, putting my hands on my head and then swiping my face with them.

"Start from that morning," she requests.

I sit up, staring at her briefly, wondering why she wants to destroy me. "Fine."

———

*I roll over to see Phoenix sprawled across her side of the bed with her hair completely covering her face. I laugh to myself, thinking how peaceful she looks, but grateful I get to wake up beside her now.*

*I have to get up extra early this morning because Braxton's on East is hosting a rehearsal dinner, and I want everything to be perfect. I tiptoe around the bed and kiss her on the forehead before walking down the hall to the other bathroom to shower and get ready.*

*She's not that sweet woman I love when you wake her up from a deep sleep. So once I realize I left my car key on the bedside table, I pick up her keys and leave a note on the kitchen counter where they were.*

*Most of the day goes pretty smoothly until the bartender starts serving the wrong drinks during the rehearsal dinner. Needless to say, the bride yells for far too long over something that could have easily been changed. Still, I remove the drinks from* the bill altogether just so she won't leave a bad review because of it.

I can't even get mad at the new bartender, Adriel, because I hired him on short notice after the one on staff never showed up today. Either way, we made it through to the dessert with no more issues. So all in all, a successful night.

"Braxton, did Nixy ever come back?" Reyna asks.

I don't know how they became so chummy in such a short period of time, but she and Phoenix have become inseparable.

"She was here?" I ask, handing the waiter the last of the chocolate lava cake.

"Yeah, she was headed back here for you and then ran right back out. I thought maybe she forgot something."

I pull out my phone, thinking she may have texted me, and it was too loud in the kitchen to hear such a faint notification. But there's nothing.

"Okay, well, when I get home, I'll tell her you were looking for her."

She smiles as she throws on her jacket to leave. I decide to let her go home, and I'll close up since she has been working so hard on this rehearsal dinner. It isn't our first but dealing with brides is hard-ass work, and they can ruin your reputation. It's not until I actually start closing out the sales and inventory that I realize why I never do this anymore.

It's about two a.m. when I finally head home. I'm sure Phoenix is dead asleep by now, so I'll have to talk to her in the morning about why she disappeared. But, I wasn't worried because she tends to not bother me while I'm working a busy dinner service. As I park the car, however, I hear my phone go off, and it's her.

**I'm sorry.**

Sorry for what? It was then I noticed my Cayenne was not in its parking spot right next to mine. I'm not sure how I didn't catch that right away. My mind jumps to her possibly wrecking my car, so I call her twice with no answer.

Fuck! GPS ...

I scroll to my car's app and pull up the location. "Her parents' house," I say aloud. That's shocking, considering she hasn't really spoken to them since she moved in with me. The words of her text keep churning in my head like a mental Rolodex, and I hope she's not sorry for what I think she's decided.

To leave me. To go back to the life she knows.

I can't have that. She deserves so much more. I throw her much slower car in reverse to back out of my extra spot, then drive out of there as fast as I can to save the woman I love from making a huge mistake. She gave me absolutely no clue that she wasn't happy. That she couldn't just trust that her parents would eventually come around. But why couldn't she have talked to me about it first? Don't I deserve even that?

No! I'm getting her out of that fucking house!

It seemed to take forever before I made it to Potomac. But as soon as I pull in front of the house, an eerie feeling falls over me. I jump out of her still-running car and peer up to her bedroom. The only thing I notice is a very dim light with some sort of swaying shadow within it. I run up the stairs and bang on the door. I don't care who answers ... I'm pushing my way in.

Something's wrong. My heart drops to the ground and everything starts spinning. Finally, her brute, Bear, answers the door.

Immediately, I punch him in the face, knowing he wouldn't let me in willingly. As he falls to the floor, I run through the door and past her parents, who come walking into the foyer from the living room, concerned about the commotion.

Her father utters some stupid threat, but that doesn't keep my feet from flying upstairs to her room as if they have a mind of their own. I hear the heavy feet of, I assume, her father close on my heels as I barge into Phoenix's room.

The first things I see are her legs, dangling in the middle of the room. I'm momentarily frozen in place as everything stills. The thumping of my heart pounding against my chest gets louder, the heavier my breathing gets. Panic rumbles from deep within as the urge to save my love propels me forward.

"No! Please!" I roar as I run into the room and stand on the step stool she used to hang herself, to get her down. I suddenly hear a loud shriek. A bloodcurdling sound that pierces my soul.

"You killed her!" I hear her mother as I gently lay Phoenix on her bed and try to resuscitate her. Her mother pounds on her father's chest, wailing uncontrollably. "You son of bitch! I hate you!" she exclaims.

"Please stop! Call the ambulance now!" I scream between blowing futile air into her non-responsive lungs. "Phoenix, please! Don't do this to me!" I shout, pounding on her chest, but there's nothing but dead eyes staring up at me. She's gone.

## CHAPTER FOURTEEN

### I'm Finally Free

THE TEARS FALL FROM MY EYES AND DOWN MY CHEEKS like I'm producing a waterfall of emotion. I haven't relived that moment that cognitively in so long. I never really wanted to. It was the hardest day of my life. Phoenix took part of my soul with her when she left me. Willingly. It was even more difficult because there was no note. No one knew why. So she took her life and any chance of closure with her. That made it even more devastating.

"I know that was hard, but there's more I need to tell you," West says, fumbling with the envelope she took from her desk.

I grab a Kleenex from the table beside me and wipe my eyes and face. "I'm sure you do."

"I know why she left the restaurant so abruptly," she says, handing me a piece of paper from the envelope.

"What's this?" I ask, curious.

"Phoenix sent me that. I got it two days after it happened," she admits.

I stare at her furiously then down at the folded paper with Roselyn West written in Phoenix's handwriting on the outside of it. "Is this what I think it is?"

West has had what I've wanted since the day before I started coming here. I want to get angry and lash out, but that gets nowhere with Roselyn. Besides, I obviously need to get used to women keeping shit from me. So I just open it and take a deep breath before reading the short message aloud.

> *Rose,*
>
> *I need you to do something for me that I hope you will consider. I came to the understanding that it will never matter what I want; Adriel will never allow me to enjoy life without him. I will never be free of my duties. He made that perfectly clear when I saw him bartending at Braxton's restaurant. Adriel will kill me first.*

I stop reading and look up at West for clarification. I hired her fucking fiancé. Her stalker.

"Keep reading," she asserts.

> *I cannot live this way. Please help Braxton. Help him understand. Help him move on. Help him love again. I don't care what it takes. He will need you to get through this, so he doesn't*

*think he's alone. I'm grateful to you and everything you've done and are willing to continue to do. I'm sure you'll find the right time to give him these letters.*

*- Phoenix*

I fold the paper back, and West gives me a moment to reconcile my thoughts. That letter was a lot to take in and brings up emotions I can't seem to leave behind. Animosity being the main one. Angry at everything and everyone, especially Phoenix for taking her own life. For taking my life along with it, and then placing the burden on West to clean up for her. Now I learn I brought her fear right back into her life. I feel the rage find it's way through the sadness and defeat as the tears well in my eyes.

"That son of a bitch should be dead too!" I shout without standing from the couch. Not because I didn't want to, but the weight of the world holds me down. I then realize she hasn't said a word, but blinks rapidly, obviously contemplating telling me something. "Oh just spit it the fuck out already."

She leans forward. "He's dead," she says simply.

The anger begins to subside slightly, knowing that mother fucker is dead. He deserves to be for tormenting someone so much they felt taking their own life was the only escape. But I want to know more. Need to know more.

"Okay, go on," I urge.

"He was found hanging in his bedroom." She looks down at the second envelope in her hand. "The medical examiner ruled it a suicide."

Her carefully chosen words swirl around my thoughts, wondering if she believes he was possibly murdered. "You say that as if you have suspicions concerning his death. Do you?" I ask.

"The last time her father came in, after he got the letter Phoenix wrote for him, he told me he didn't need to come back here. That he dealt with it. *An eye for an eye*, he said. Then just walked out." She takes a deep breath. "The next day, I read in the paper that he was found dead."

A passive smile forms on my face, pleased with her father finally doing something for his daughter and not worry about how it may affect him, but then I realize I now have another murder to weigh on my conscience. Another death that may not have occurred if I one, didn't make Phoenix decide to pick a future with me, and two, let Adriel work for me on short notice.

"Braxton, this is not your fault. She made her own decision, for her own reasons, and it had nothing to do with you hiring Adriel."

I drop my head. "I hear you, but that's hard to believe, considering she killed herself right after."

"So, let her tell you." West hands me the envelope, which I reluctantly take.

It's only then that I realize she said letters in the plural sense.

"I don't understand why you kept this from me," I

whisper, annoyed, but too defeated to fully express my outrage. I'm just too drained. I feel as if my insides have been completely hollowed out, and there's nothing left but the emptiness of my tarnished soul.

So, I sit back on the couch and pull the other paper out. This one isn't folded and is a bit longer. I look up at West, who stands to leave the room and gives me privacy.

*Braxton,*
*If you're reading this, then I've done something that has taken both of our lives. I know you're hurting and probably angry, but you've come so far, my love. You've learned to open your heart and let someone in. I'm honored I was the one you chose to love. To yearn for. To adore. To save. I need you to remember the Braxton you are now and not backslide. Don't do it just for me, but for your future and the woman that is lucky enough to have you. You and I both know you already met that woman, so go find her. You owe it to yourself to try. Don't harbor any anger, baby, because none of this is your fault.*
*By now, you must know that for the past three years, I've been living in fear. Fear that began with giving the rest of my life to a stranger, but eventually led to mental and physical abuse at the hands of a man placed in my life by my own father. The only solace I could find was to*

*remove myself from the tyrant that would kill me, to the tyrant I thought hated me, my father. I misled my father to believe I wasn't ready to fulfill my duty wholeheartedly, and he went for it, considering he didn't want me to embarrass him. That's until you came along. I needed to live my own life, and I wanted it to be with you. Unfortunately, I may have escaped my father's grasp, but I learned tonight I could never escape the clutches of the man that used those same hands to almost forcefully drain the life out of me. But I refuse to let Adriel take over my life again. I'm finally free.*

*Love you always,
Your Phoenix.*

I begin to sob relentlessly as every feeling I can no longer control explodes all at once. All this time, I assumed she thought so little of me that she couldn't even tell me why.

"She left one for her parents too. He came to your restaurant that day to apologize. The day you turned him away. He had no idea about Adriel beating his daughter and threatening her life constantly. Despite what Phoenix believed, he sobbed in front of me just as you're doing." She stoops down in front of me and hands me another Kleenex. "Do you know why?"

I shake my head, unable to speak.

"Because he just let his ego get in the way. He couldn't honestly say if he would've made Phoenix marry Adriel anyway."

"So, she was right. She had no chance of being with me and having her family," I lower my head, "but that still doesn't excuse it."

"And nothing would." She grabs my hands, which are still gripping the letter. "The point is, are you going to let your ego get in the way? We both know you're going to be a good father to that little boy."

"I absolutely will."

"Can you honestly say you're not in love with Senara? That you can move on from her?"

I think before I answer for once. The anger in me wants to say fuck her. I don't need to be in a relationship with her to have one with my son. But the other half of me, the part of me that Phoenix helped me find, wants to be with her. In every way possible. If I'm really truthful with myself, if she tried contacting me before, I'm not sure if I would've responded.

"No, I can't," I whisper.

"Then you know what you have to do." She stands, backing away from me.

I get up from the couch with purpose, smiling as I shift my clothes and adjust myself before I walk toward the door, but stop in the doorway. "Thank you, Roselyn."

It takes me all of thirty minutes before I'm back at the Renae house. I look at the clock to make sure it's not too late before I get out of the car and knock on the door. A tall, grey-haired man answers.

"I'm glad you came back, son," he says, extending his hand. "I'm Blake Renae, Senara's father."

I smile wide, happily shaking his hand and glad to see I don't have to deal with another father hating me right off the bat. It seems Senara has already told him all about me too, which shouldn't be a surprise considering my son is living here.

"I am too, sir."

"Come in." He steps back for me to walk in their quaint, homey foyer. It's not long before I step into the hall that I hear a woman's voice that isn't Senara.

"See, I told you, Renae," she says, wagging her finger at Mr. Renae, with her other hand on her hip. She walks right up to me and gives me a hug. "Good to see ya, Suga." She takes a step back and holds my face in her hands. "Oh, you're so handsome too. Good thing my grandson has your looks." She giggles as she drops her hands to my arms. "I'm sorry it took so long for my daughter to tell you, but you can't live your kids' lives for them. They have to make their own decisions."

I nod, knowing she's right and happy this is the home my son has been growing up in.

"Braxton," Senara appears behind her mother, holding Little Braxton, who appears to be dead asleep in his pajamas. Tears well in Sen's eyes as her mother moves from between us.

"Is it his bedtime?" I ask, and she only nods. "May I?" I

point at my son, implying that I'd like to put him to bed. Something I'd be doing for the first time, but how hard could it be?

She walks over to me and lets me take him into my arms. He lifts his head slightly, seeing the strange man from earlier is now holding him, but he only smiles slightly and then drops his head on my shoulder.

"Up the stairs, on the left," Mrs. Renae offers before I can ask.

I slowly walk up the stairs, trying not to wake him. I make it to his Batman-decorated bedroom and pull the covers back in his racecar bed. I carefully place him in the bed and pull the covers up, before kneeling at his bedside.

"I'm sorry I missed the beginning of your life. But I promise, I'll be here every day from this day forward, Lil' Man," I whisper. I watch him sleep for a while, wishing I could just stay here, but I know I have to go. But I'll make it a point to be here first thing in the morning.

I make my way downstairs only to find Sen alone in the kitchen washing dishes. I stare at her briefly, knowing I could never live another day without her now. Although she made an irreparable mistake, there is no one worth forgiving than the mother of my child.

I quietly ease up behind her and wrap my arms around her waist. She tries to turn, but I hold her in place.

"Braxton, I never meant to—"

"Shh ..." I bend down so that she can hear me clearly, "thank you for taking care of our son." I hear her sniffling. "Now it's my turn to take care of both of you." I spin her around and quickly begin to kiss her as if there's no tomorrow, and this connection is keeping us alive. All I need is to feel her lips against mine. To feel the touch that has already begun to fill the soul that was hollowed hours before. I know this is where I belong, with my second chance at living a fulfilled, joyous life. I may have had to go through hell to get here, but I was allowed to find my own freedom because of it. Without one ounce of animosity, I utter the three words I've known I felt all those years ago. I place my forehead on hers, "I love you."

"I love you too."

The End:

Subscribe to the Hotness

Meet the next Internet Famous Celeb in DEVOTED.

# INTERNET FAMOUS COLLECTION

Whether they accidentally rose to fame or staked the claim, these modern-day princes are social media royalty. Follow the Internet famous celebs as they deal with fame, power, and the consequences of falling in love. Each story is a STANDALONE fairytale retelling with an HEA and swoon-worthy alphas. There's a little something for every book craving.

✔ Sonya Jesus's twisted retelling of Cinderella brings to life a fairytale killer obsessed with a True Crime Blogger and her Internet famous crush in SHOOK.

## INTERNET FAMOUS COLLECTION

✓ Mel Walker livens up the stage with his Princess and the Pea retelling, which combines music and dance into the beat of love. STAGEFIGHT.

✓ Nancy Chastain's friends-to-lovers, sports romance, BEAST, follows the MMA fighter and his first love in a page-turning Beauty and the Beast retelling.

✓ Tasha Lewis's Little Mermaid retelling follows the prince of the ocean on his shipwrecked voyage in DESERTED, a contemporary romance that gives love a voice.

✓ Maree Moon's Arabian Night retelling combines sweet romance and accidental fame, turning the Internet into the genie of love and romance into a chanced encounter. CHANCED.

✓ Cam Johns's dark retelling of Rapunzel is a second chance romance that will leave you craving more from this hot celebrity chef and salivating for SECONDS.

✓ Jade Royal's lesbian romance changes up The Legend of Hua Mulan, defying the rules of gender identity, war, and the Internet by a girl more DEVOTED to win than her contenders.

✓ MK Moore's Snow White retelling is a steamy contemporary romance about the gamer celebrity and the girl who TROLLED him.

www.rewrittenfairytales.com

G E T M O R E I N F O :

www.facebook.com/rewrittenfairytales

S U B S C R I B E to the Hotness:

http://eepurl.com/gYEHqL

# ALSO BY CAM JOHNS

**Book Links: The Arousing Series**

1. Arousing Consequences - My Book

2. Arousing Secrets - My Book

3. Arousing Inferno - My Book

4. Two to the Back (Escaping the Mafia)- My Book

5. Midnight Princess (Modern Princess Collection) - My Book

# ABOUT THE AUTHOR

Cam Johns began her career as a published author in 2016 with the release of her first book – Arousing Consequences – to the three-part series, The Arousing Series. However, actually publishing wasn't part of her plan. After her husband was diagnosed with Multiple Sclerosis, she found that writing became a great way to relieve the tension and mounted pressures that come with watching someone she loves suffer from such a harsh diagnosis. It was her husband that pushed her to share her voice, regardless of how erotic that voice would become.

Live. Love. Laugh.

A well-known mantra that has become my way of living. Live, by accepting the things you cannot change. Love, the ones closest to you as if there's no tomorrow. Laugh, each day because sadness will get you nowhere!

**Social Links:**
Website – www.thecamjohns.com
Facebook Group – www.facebook.com/groups/CamSquad
Newsletter - http://eepurl.com/dsiCRT